THE
SAVAGE
TRAIL

CHARLES E. FRIEND

Fithian Press

SANTA BARBARA

1992

Design and typography by Jim Cook

Published by Fithian Press
Post Office Box 1525
Santa Barbara, CA 93120

LIBRARY OF CONGRESS CATALOGING-IN-PUBLICATION DATA
Friend, Charles E.
The savage trail: a novel / Charles E. Friend.
p. cm.
ISBN 1-56474-043-9
I. Title.
PS3556.R5663S28   1992
813'.54 dc20   92-33213
CIP

THE
SAVAGE
TRAIL

"Before seeking vengeance, dig two graves."

—OLD PROVERB

CHAPTER ONE

Starbuck saw the smoke about midday. The jagged hills ahead hid the flames from his view, but he knew immediately that it was Comanche Wells. Nothing else lay beyond those buttes that would make a blaze that big; the smoke had drifted up a thousand feet or more, staining the clear desert air a greasy black. The town—his town—was burning.

His horse was already tired from the morning's ride, but Starbuck immediately spurred the animal into a dead run. He left the trail and rode cross-country, desperate to reach the source of that ugly smear against the sky. Heedless of the risk to the horse and himself, he charged headlong over the rough ground, dodging through the tall saguaro cactus and plunging across the soft sand of the dry washes without slackening the pace. A mile, a mile and a half, and the big sorrel began to falter from sheer exhaustion. Starbuck drove the horse onward, shouting encouragement to him as they raced through the brush.

They clattered up the last rise, the horse fighting to keep its footing on the slippery rocks. At the crest of the hill Starbuck reined in, staring at the valley below.

There was little left of Comanche Wells. Stores, offices, houses, barns—almost all were gone. In their place there were only charred ruins, some of them still burning. And more than the buildings had gone; even from the rise a half-mile away, Starbuck could see bodies sprawled in the streets.

He rode in past the smoldering remains of the feed and grain store, the stage office, the assay office. The livery stable was intact, but the rails of the corral were down and there were no horses to be seen. The livery stable owner lay dead beside the stable door.

A few yards further along the street, Starbuck paused in front of the blackened remnants of the hotel. Three more corpses were huddled there in the dust—two men and a woman. All three had been shot in the back of the head. The woman's body was only partly clothed.

The hitch rail in front of the marshal's office was still standing, and Starbuck tied the horse to it. The office had been burned, but the jail behind it was unharmed. Its adobe walls had resisted the fire.

Someone shouted "Marshal!" and Starbuck turned. Frank Hardesty, the blacksmith, was running toward him, a rifle in his hand.

"Thank God you're back," Hardesty cried.

"What happened here, Frank?" Starbuck rasped, slipping the Winchester out of his saddle scabbard. "Who did this? Damn it, man, speak up!"

"Bandits," said Hardesty. "They hit us a couple of hours ago. Looted everything in sight, shot anybody who got in their way. Look, there's Freeman!"

Another man was running toward them, and Starbuck saw that it was indeed Jess Freeman, the owner of the general store. His clothes were in tatters and his skin was scorched, as if he had just escaped from one of the burning buildings. As he reached Starbuck and Hardesty he went down onto his knees, his breath coming in ragged gasps.

"Who was it, Jess?" Starbuck said, helping him up.

Freeman shook his head.

"Never saw them before, any of them."

"Indians?"

"No, white men. A few Mexicans. My God, Grant, they

tore the place apart, took anything they wanted. Got the bank first, then the rest of the town. Then they began to set fire to everything. When people ran out of the burning buildings they shot them down."

He closed his eyes, and his face twisted in anguish.

"My wife—she was in the store when they came. They . . . they *took* her, one after the other, and then shot her, right there in front of me. Then they set fire to the store. I barely got out."

He put his hands over his eyes and began to cry.

"I went to the school to find little Jess," he sobbed. "The schoolhouse was on fire too. Can you believe it? They even set fire to the school!"

"The children," said Starbuck hoarsely. "What happened to the children?"

"I don't know. Maybe they ran away. I couldn't find my boy."

Cold fear suddenly gripped Grant Starbuck.

"My family, Jess? Did you see my wife, my boys?"

"No . . . no, I didn't. I'm sorry. Oh, God, Marshal, there's hardly anybody left alive!"

With a curse, Starbuck tore the sorrel's reins free of the hitchrail and swung into the saddle. He raced down the street through the pall of drifting smoke, ignoring the burning wreckage and the scattered bodies. As he rode, his smarting eyes searched desperately ahead for the familiar picket fence and whitewashed walls of his house. The destruction had so altered the appearance of the town that at first he wasn't certain of his bearings, and when he came to the street where he lived he had to pull the horse up and orient himself in order to find his home.

Then he saw it . . . or what was left of it. The picket fence was still there, but the house was gone. Only the same pitiful pile of charred wood and ashes which marked the rest of Comanche Wells awaited him where once his home had stood.

Frantically he looked around. Across the street an elderly woman was sitting on the ground, her back propped against a tree. She seemed to be unconscious. He dismounted and knelt beside her.

"Mrs. Johnson," he said, shaking her. "Are you all right?"

She opened her eyes and gazed blankly at him.

"Marshal," she said at last. "Thank Heaven you're here. Those men . . ."

"My wife and children, Mrs. Johnson. Have you seen them?"

"Yes," she mumbled. "Yes, I saw them . . ."

"Where are they, Mrs. Johnson?"

Her lips moved, but at first no sound emerged. Then she pointed toward the ruins of his house.

"There," she whispered. "They're over there."

He hurried back across the street. The useless gate was standing open and he ran through it, right up to the edge of the still-hot ashes where the house had been.

Then he saw them—three blackened, shrivelled forms lying tangled in the smoking wreckage, barely recognizable as having once been human. One of the bodies was larger than the others; its arms were wrapped around the smaller two, as if trying to protect them.

Grant Starbuck spun away, retching violently. At last, the spasm over, he slowly straightened up and stood for a long time staring blindly at the sky. Tears coursed down his cheeks. He had not thought that it was possible to feel such pain.

Slowly the surviving citizens of Comanche Wells came out of hiding. Dazed and angry, they told their stories to each other and to Grant Starbuck.

There had been at least twenty-five men, perhaps thirty. They had ridden in out of the south with guns blazing, shooting people down in the street without provocation or warning. A few of the townspeople had fought back, firing at the attackers from windows and doorways, but the defenders were too few and most of them were just clerks and storekeepers, ill-prepared for a battle with hardened gunmen. Within minutes all resistance had been crushed.

The raiders had then begun to loot, taking the money from the bank, rifling the stores, even stripping rings and other valuables from the bodies in the street. When a man was found hiding in the buildings, he was shot. The women were not always so fortunate; some, like Jess Freeman's wife, had been raped where they were found, then brutally murdered. Others were taken captive and dragged away at the end of a rope when the outlaws finally rode off, leaving the town in flames.

Starbuck spent an hour listening to the tales of horror. From each survivor he tried to get a description of the attackers, but all that he could learn was that they had been white men, not Indians, and that several had been Mexicans or at least had been dressed in the Mexican style. They had all been well armed and were riding good horses. One of them, possibly the leader, had been a tall, thin man dressed in black; everyone remembered that he had a huge scar across his cheek. Of the rest, Starbuck could get no useful description from the shocked, terrified victims of the attack. All that anyone could say for certain was that when the marauders had tired of looting, raping, and killing, they had rounded up all of the horses in town and then driven them off southward toward the Mexican border.

Presently one of the stolen horses came wandering back into town with a broken bridle; Starbuck put Frank Hardesty on its back and sent him off to summon the Army from Fort Scott, twenty miles away. Then he began to search for survivors in the ruins.

There were more than he had expected. Some people had hidden in outbuildings or run away into the desert and so had avoided the fate of those less quick-witted or less fortunate.

But there were many dead. Starbuck counted seventeen corpses in the streets, twenty-eight more in the ashes of the burned buildings. Most of the school-age children had survived; they had fled into the underbrush when the raiders fired the schoolhouse.

The schoolteacher and six other women were missing.

Among the survivors was Doc Harper, the town's physician. He had been at an outlying ranch delivering a baby when the attack came, and had rushed back when he heard the gunfire and saw the smoke. Starbuck helped him with some of the injured.

"I can't believe it," Harper growled as he bandaged a little girl's burned face. "There hasn't been a raid like this around here in ten years. Not since the Comanches were cleared out. Apaches used to come over the border occasionally, but those were just small raids on isolated ranches. Nothing like this."

Starbuck knelt down beside the sobbing child to comfort her. His face was gray with strain and weariness.

"I did hear of one raid something like this one," he said to Harper. "It was about six months ago, just over the line in New Mexico. The Army chased them south toward the border but they got away."

"Indians?"

"No, supposedly Mexican bandits did it."

"Think it was the same bunch that hit us?"

"I don't know, Doc. I wish I did. I wish I'd paid more attention when I heard about it. And I wish to God that I'd been here this morning."

Harper snorted.

"It wouldn't have made any difference. You'd just have been killed trying to stop 'em."

"That's not the point."

"Oh? What is the point then?"

"This is my town, Doc," Starbuck said bitterly. "These people counted on me to protect them. That's my job. I was supposed to keep them safe. I was supposed to keep my family safe, too. Now. . . ."

His voice broke. He got up and walked away.

Thirty minutes later he was resaddling the sorrel. The animal was tired, for Starbuck had been out since dawn trailing some steers that had been reported rustled in the hills to the west of Comanche Wells. That errand had saved Starbuck's life, but the long ride and the hard dash back to town had left him with a worn-out horse, and there were no others left in Comanche Wells; the raiders had taken them all, driving the animals before them as they rode out. The sorrel would have to do. Starbuck rubbed the horse down, fed and watered him, then put the saddle back on and cinched up.

Doc Harper appeared as he was tying his bedroll to the saddle.

"What are you going to do?" Harper asked.

Starbuck slid his Winchester into the saddle scabbard.

"I'm going to get them, Doc. Every one of them, if God lets me live that long."

"Good grief, man," said the doctor, "there are two or three dozen of them, and you'll be alone. Send someone to the Fort for the soldiers."

"I did. It'll take them too long to get here."

"But. . . ."

Starbuck swung into the saddle.

"You still don't understand, Doc," he said heavily. "This is *my* town, not the Army's. These are . . . were . . . my people. My home. My family. My responsibility. Mine, not the Army's. The soldiers will bring tents, supplies, maybe another doctor to help you. That's their job. Getting the swine who did this is up to me."

"You damn fool," Harper cried, "you haven't got a chance."

"I know," Starbuck said, gathering up the reins. "But that doesn't matter now. I should have died here on this street when those killers rode in this morning, died right here along with my family and all the others. At least I could have taken some of the murdering bastards with me. Well, this way maybe I still can."

Harper shook his head slowly. He was not an emotional man, but he was a little frightened by what he saw in Starbuck's eyes.

"Good luck, son," he said, his voice trembling.

"Good-bye, Doc."

Starbuck checked to see that the marshal's star was pinned firmly in place on his shirt, then swung the sorrel's head around and trotted out of town toward the south, following the tracks of his quarry.

CHAPTER TWO

The marauders had ridden straight for the border, making no attempt to cover their tracks. Suppressing the urge to spur the sorrel into a gallop, Starbuck put the animal into a slow trot instead, watching the trail and the land ahead. The raiders might leave a few men behind as a rear guard, and it would be foolish to charge into an ambush. Above all, he must not founder the horse; left afoot in the desert he would be as good as dead, and even if he survived the killers would escape.

Besides, there was no reason for blind haste. He could not expect to catch up to the raiders before dark in any event—their lead was too great—but if he kept up a steady pace he could hope to overtake them by morning. Their tracks told him that they were not moving very rapidly. They must know that the Army would come after them, but they must also know that it would be hours before the Fort could be alerted, and days, perhaps, before the cavalry could catch up to them.

In addition, they were pushing many horses. Comanche Wells was a way station where the stage line kept fresh teams for the stagecoaches, and the livery stable owner always had extra horses on hand for sale to the Army. The presence of so many valuable animals might be the very reason why the raiders had selected Comanche Wells as their target. If so, they must be well pleased with their haul, for they had seized a fair-sized herd. But driving it would slow them down.

And then, of course, there were the women.

He found the first body five miles south of Comanche Wells. He would not have noticed her had he not seen the torn dress caught in a patch of cholla cactus a hundred feet off the trail. The flutter of blue calico caught his eye, and when he rode over to examine the dress he saw the body lying in a wash below him. It was the schoolteacher. When they had finished with her they had put a bullet between her eyes, but from the appearance of the body and the gunshot wound itself Starbuck guessed that she had been dead long before the shot was fired.

He would have liked to bury her, but he dared not delay that long. It seemed callous just to leave her there, but he reminded himself that she was past caring and that there were living hostages ahead who might still be saved if help arrived in time. As he rode back up out of the wash, a buzzard started to circle lazily overhead, quickly joined by another. Starbuck knew that as soon as he was gone they would begin to tear at the woman's body. He set his jaw and started south again, this time riding a little faster.

An hour out of Comanche Wells the trail began to climb into some low hills, passing between two buttes that rose high above the track on either side. Any rider coming through this narrow defile would be an easy target. Starbuck decided that if he were on the run through this country and wanted to leave a rear guard behind to discourage pursuit, he would do it here. Yet the tracks he was following led straight up between those buttes. To go around would take hours, and the sun was already halfway down the western sky. He decided to risk it.

He slowed the sorrel to a walk and slid the Winchester out of the scabbard, laying it across the saddle in front of him. His eyes searched the skyline restlessly for any sign of danger.

When it came, it came abruptly. Far up in the rocks at the base of the left-hand butte he saw a brief glint of sunlight on steel, followed immediately by a puff of smoke. The sound of the shot reached him just as the bullet struck the sorrel; the slug made a sickening, liquid noise as it took the animal full in the chest. The horse pitched forward onto its knees and then slumped slowly over into the dust, already dead.

As the sorrel fell Starbuck kicked free of the stirrups and hit the ground running. From the slopes a second rifle fired at him; the bullet kicked up dirt between his boots. He threw himself headlong into a small gully next to the trail, keeping a tight grip on the Winchester as he fell. The impact with the hard earth drove the breath from his body and cactus raked his flesh as he rolled over into firing position, the rifle already lined up on the spot in the rocks from which the gunfire had come. He snapped two quick shots into the area to keep the drygulchers' heads down, then scrambled a dozen yards up the slope and into the shelter of a large boulder. He huddled there in the shadow of the rock, gasping for breath.

The minutes passed. He waited tensely, searching the rocks for some movement, some target, but he could see nothing. The gunsmoke from the initial shots had now blown away in the wind. Gradually his breathing slowed to normal, and he settled down to wait in the heat. The flat rock upon which he crouched was as hot as a skillet in the desert sun.

"Hey, amigo," a voice called from the slope. "Hope you got plenty of water down there, 'cause we're gonna be here a long time."

Starbuck looked back at the dead sorrel lying in the trail. His canteen was still looped over the saddle horn. There was no way that he could reach it alive.

"Just take your time, amigo," the voice said. "Now us, we got lots of water. We even got a woman up here to keep us company. Here, I'll let her talk to you."

There was a moment's pause, and then a shrill scream of agony echoed between the buttes.

"Come on up, amigo," called the voice. "We'll share her with you!"

Another shriek came out of the rocks. It rose to a horrid crescendo and then tapered off into a long, animal-like howl. Starbuck writhed impotently behind the rock, biting his lip so hard that it bled. They were trying to goad him into charging up the slope at them, and he must not fall into the trap.

He edged around the back side of the boulder and surveyed the terrain above him. The men in the rocks had chosen a good position, but Starbuck knew this country well; a dozen years before he had fought Comanches among these same buttes, and he knew that there was an arroyo to his left that would take him up the base of the butte without exposing him to the rifle fire from above. His knowledge of the ground gave him an edge, and it was time for him to use it.

Quickly he slid back down the rock face and, cradling the Winchester in his arms, wormed his way across a patch of shale to a low depression in the ground out of the ambushers' line of sight. Reaching down, he slipped off his spurs and tossed them into the brush. Then he was on his feet, running up the small defile through the rocks, praying that they would not hear him as he ran.

Two quick shots cracked out, but the bullets passed well away from him, striking the area where he had first leaped from the dying horse. They had not seen him move.

"Hey, amigo," called the same voice, "the lady here wants to sing you a song. Sing for our amigo, honey!"

This time the scream went on and on. Starbuck drove himself up through the rocks like a man possessed until he reached the rim just above the level from which the shots had come; then he began to work his way along the ledge toward the pitiful sounds rising from among the rocks. Twice his boots slipped, sending little showers of dirt and pebbles down the hill, but the screams covered the noise.

Slowly he raised his head up over the rimrock and found himself looking down into a small natural pocket in the boulders.

One of the ambushers was stretched out among the rocks, peering over them at the trail below with his rifle at the ready. The other man was standing immediately below Starbuck, straddling the body of a woman. The second man had a bloody bowie knife in his hand, and Starbuck could see that the woman's flesh had been slashed in a dozen places.

"Hey," said the man with the knife to his companion, "you get that hombre yet?"

"Naw," said the other, "can't get a clear shot at him."

"Well," said the one with the knife, "we can't wait here forever. We got to get goin' pretty quick if we're gonna catch up with the rest by dark. Anyway, I think this bitch is dead. She don't scream no more when I stick the knife in her. Here, I'll show ya."

He poised the knife for another thrust. Starbuck raised the Winchester in one smooth motion and shot him through the head. He collapsed like a poleaxed steer on top of the woman, the knife flying off among the rocks.

The other man scrambled frantically out of his prone position, stark terror on his face as he tried to bring his rifle up to fire, knowing that it was hopeless. Starbuck's shot took him in the belly, knocking him back against the rocks. He groaned once and then slid down into a crumpled heap, the rifle sliding slowly out of his dying fingers. Starbuck shot him again, this time in the chest, then leaped down into the depression. He kicked the corpse off the woman's mutilated body and bent over her, then quickly stood up and turned away. She was beyond help.

Carefully and deliberately, Starbuck drew his six-gun and put five rounds into the dead knife-wielder's face.

Working rapidly, he stripped the dead gunmen of their weapons and ammunition. One of the rifles was an old Henry, and he smashed it against a rock. The other rifle was a Winchester, and both men were carrying six-guns; all of these he took. In a matter of minutes he had located their horses tethered farther back among the rocks. One of the animals was a bay gelding with a bad limp from a stone bruise on his hoof. Starbuck unsaddled him and turned him loose. The other horse was a gray mare which rolled her eyes and reared as Starbuck approached. He removed the silver-ornamented saddle from her back and placed it on the ground near the gear which he had taken from the gelding. A quick search of the two sets of saddlebags produced over two hundred dollars in cash and a small leather bag containing several ounces of gold dust and four gold wedding rings—loot from the Comanche Wells raid. One of the rings still had a finger in it. Apparently the man who had taken it had been in a hurry.

Gathering up the dead men's canteens, Starbuck led the mare down to the trail where the sorrel was lying. He took his saddle, bridle, saddlebags, and bedroll from the dead animal and placed them on the mare. He slipped the extra six-guns and ammunition into the saddlebags and tied the additional Winchester behind the saddle. Then he retrieved his spurs from the underbrush and mounted up. The mare danced sideways as he settled into the saddle; he calmed the animal with the ease of long experience. A moment later he was moving up the trail through the buttes at a canter. As he passed over the crest he glanced back and saw that once again the buzzards were gathering.

The sun was setting now, a typical desert sunset filled with bright streaks of orange and brilliant shades of red. To Starbuck's fevered imagination it seemed that the light that touched the buttes around him was painting the land with blood. He rode on, mentally and physically exhausted, with the smell of death in his nostrils and the images of death in his mind. After the horror of that long afternoon, he wondered if he would ever be free of either of them again.

CHAPTER THREE

For another hour he trailed southward. As the short desert twilight faded into darkness it became more difficult to follow the raiders' tracks, but as Starbuck crossed a wide dry wash there was still enough light for him to see that the men that he was pursuing had abruptly split into two groups. He dismounted and examined the soft sand closely, not daring to light a match. Even in the near-dark, however, it was apparent that one group had continued to push the stolen horse herd south while the second party, five or six of them, had turned off to the southwest.

He stood holding the mare's reins, trying to guess the reason for the split-up. Then, as he gazed out at the shadowy land before him, he saw the reason. Through the cactus and underbrush a flicker of light was visible. It was a light all too easily recognizable for what it was—the glow of burning timbers. There was no town nearby, so it could only be someone's ranch. And the tracks showed that the second group of raiders had headed in that direction.

Starbuck moved through the darkness at a slow walk, alert for any sign that the raiders might still be near. Only the normal sounds of night in the desert broke the stillness. The fire was closer now, and he could see the outline of a windmill burning. Ranches in that area had to pump their water from far beneath the ground, so the ranchers often erected windmills to do the pumping. This one had been set afire, and the wooden portions were almost burned away. Only the metal parts remained, some of them still glowing red from the heat.

He dismounted and tethered the mare in the brush, drew his ivory-handled Colt, and moved forward through the night toward the glow in front of him. One final clump of brush separated him from it; he slid soundlessly around the tangled growth and knelt down in the shadows.

It was indeed a ranch, or had been. The main building was made of adobe and so had not been consumed by the fire, but the outbuildings had been burned; the stable was still burning, in fact. The flickering firelight revealed a welter of smashed furniture and torn clothing strewn in the cleared area in front of the house. Near the door a human form lay stretched upon the ground. Someone had covered the body with a blanket—two boots protruded from beneath its edge.

Starbuck cocked the six-gun and moved forward, peering about the circle of light. There was no one else to be seen, but there were many hoofprints in the dust and enough light for him to see what the fire and the destruction and the corpse had already told him. The Comanche Wells murderers had made another stop on their way south, and had claimed another victim.

Yet there must be someone else about, for the dead man had surely not covered himself with the blanket, and it hardly seemed likely that the raiders had done it. Standing in the circle of firelight Starbuck would be plainly visible to any watcher, but he was not unduly alarmed. The raiders would be long gone; he could see the tracks leading out of the light toward the southeast, so anyone left on the scene would be a survivor of the attack.

"Hello, the house!" he called.

"Drop it!" said a female voice behind him. He started to turn, then froze as he felt the unmistakable shape of a gun muzzle thrust hard against his spine.

"Drop it, damn you!" the woman behind him snarled. He carefully uncocked the Colt and let it fall into the dirt.

"It's all right, ma'am," he said. "I'm . . ."

"Shut up. Now turn around, slowly. One wrong move and I'll cut you in half with this scattergun."

He turned and found himself staring down the twin barrels of a twelve-gauge shotgun. The woman holding it was tall, almost as tall as Starbuck, with a long mane of auburn hair which gleamed copper-red in the firelight. Her green eyes were sunken and tired but they flashed fire at him, and he could see that she was trembling as she covered him with the shotgun.

"Who are you, mister? Talk fast!"

"I'm Grant Starbuck, Marshal of Comanche Wells. I saw the flames from the trail."

"Marshal?" she said, her eyes dropping to the star on his shirt. "Starbuck . . . Comanche Wells. Yes . . . yes, I've heard of you."

She lowered the shotgun, easing down the cocked hammers.

"I'm sorry, Marshal," she said. "I thought you were one of . . . them."

"You haven't told me your name," he said.

"I'm Kate Beaumont," she replied. "That's my husband, Tom, over there under the blanket. They killed him."

She was trembling in earnest now, her whole body shaking as if with the palsy. Starbuck took the shotgun gently from her and put his arm around her; she sagged against him, then put her hands over her face and began to cry.

Well, Starbuck told himself, at least this one's still alive.

Kate Beaumont refused to go back into the house, so he retrieved some blankets from among the debris inside, spread them on the earth at the far edge of the firelight, and made her sit down. She sank to the ground almost gratefully, her strength spent. He left the shotgun beside her while he went back into the brush to bring up the mare.

When he had re-tethered the animal close by he went to the water tank which stood beneath the smoldering windmill. Although the pump and windmill were destroyed the tank was intact and the water clear, so he drew some for the horse, for Kate Beaumont, and for himself.

Then he sat beside her on the blankets while she told him a story which now seemed fearfully familiar. The raiders had come suddenly out of the brush, shooting. She and her husband had been eating supper when it began; her husband had pushed her into the root cellar beneath the house, then seized his rifle and tried to defend his home. Half stunned by the fall down the cellar steps, she had heard it all—the gunfire, the ugly sound of bullets striking flesh, her husband's scream, and then nothing but the gleeful shouts of the raiders as they sacked the house, fired the outbuildings, and rode away. Somehow they had not noticed the root cellar door, and so her life was spared. But in ten short minutes her home, her marriage, all of the things that she had lived for and worked to build—all had been destroyed.

By the time that she had finished her account of the raid the fire had died out. The moon had not yet risen, but the sky was clear and in the starlight they could plainly see the ruined buildings, the prized belongings broken and strewn about, the still form beneath the blanket by the door.

The windmill finally collapsed in one last shower of sparks, and Kate Beaumont's last reserves of strength fell with it. She clung to Starbuck and cried bitterly, her body shuddering with grief and the after-effects of terror. He drew a blanket around her to protect her from the chill of the desert night, then held her close beside him through the long hours. He was uncomfortable sitting there with his arm about this grief-stricken stranger, and he was desperately anxious to resume the pursuit of the murderers he had been dogging. But he knew that he could not just ride off into the darkness and leave this woman alone in that shadowy place of death and broken dreams. And so he stayed. Toward morning Kate Beaumont slept, her head on Starbuck's shoulder.

Starbuck did not sleep. Even as he held the sleeping woman he remained painfully awake, nursing his own grief, thinking of his dead wife and children, his dead neighbors, and his looted, gutted town. And all through those endless hours his hollow, burning eyes remained wide open, fixed unwaveringly on the southern horizon.

CHAPTER FOUR

At dawn Starbuck roused the woman from her fitful sleep. He found a shovel in the remains of the stable, and together they buried her husband in a shallow grave behind the house. In the wreckage of the kitchen they found enough unspoiled food to make a passable breakfast, although neither of them felt much like eating. Afterwards, he saddled the gray mare. Kate Beaumont watched, her face drawn and haggard.

"What are you going to do now, Marshal?" she said.

"Every hour the men who murdered your husband and my family are getting further and further away. I'm going after them."

"And leave me here?"

"I'm sorry, but I have no choice."

"I want to go with you," she said.

"You can't. You have no horse."

"We can ride double."

"Mrs. Beaumont," he said patiently, "these men are headed for Mexico. Once they're over the border, they'll be traveling through some of the roughest country in the world. This mare will be lucky to make it just carrying one person, let alone two."

"All right," she said, "then take me to the trading post at Indian Springs. The agent there will sell me a horse."

"And then?"

"Then I'll go where I please."

Starbuck hesitated. Indian Springs was off to the southeast. If the raiders held to their southerly track, taking Kate Beaumont to the trading post would cost him valuable time. He would have to ride back many miles to pick up the outlaws' trail.

Yet he realized that even in broad daylight he could not simply abandon her, afoot and alone, in this isolated spot. A woman by herself in such circumstances would be in great danger. He had found her alive; he must keep her that way. The pursuit would have to wait. No matter, he decided. In the end he would get them anyway, whatever the delay.

"Indian Springs it is then," he said.

They came to Indian Springs in the late morning. They walked in, with Starbuck leading the gray mare. At first they had ridden double, but as the mare began to tire Starbuck had announced that he would walk for awhile to relieve the animal of its double burden. To his amazement Kate Beaumont had promptly dismounted also, refusing to ride while he walked. Consequently they were both afoot when they came over the rise that overlooked the trading post.

The post itself was nothing more than a single large adobe structure flanked by a few dilapidated outbuildings. Its windows were mere vertical slits, reminders of an earlier day when windows in that part of the country had to be used as firing points to fight off Indian attacks. A man named Otto Baltz ran the place; his avarice was legendary. Starbuck had met him once and did not look forward to renewing the acquaintance. The best that could be said of Baltz was that he treated everyone, whites and Indians alike, with equal dishonesty. Starbuck disliked the thought of having to deal with him. Yet as they came down the hill he saw that there were several horses in the corral and two at the hitch rail in front of the store. With a little luck they could procure a horse for Kate Beaumont and she could go her way, leaving him free to resume his pursuit.

As he tied up the mare he glanced casually over at the other two horses tied to the hitch rail. Suddenly his eyes narrowed— one of the horses seemed familiar. He walked over to the animal and inspected it carefully, suppressing a growing excitement. It was the big buckskin stallion which had been the pride and joy of Nate Wilson, the livery stable owner in Comanche Wells. It had been taken by the raiders the day before . . . after they had shot its owner dead in the street.

Starbuck looked quickly at the trading post, wondering if anyone inside had seen him examining the horse.

Kate Beaumont sensed his sudden tautness.

"What's the matter?" she said.

"This horse was stolen from Comanche Wells yesterday," he said. "I recognize it."

She stared at him, her eyes wide.

He checked the cylinder of his Colt Peacemaker and slid it back into the holster, leaving the rawhide thong off the hammer. Then he unpinned his marshal's star and slid it into his shirt pocket.

"Wait here for me," he said to the woman. "I'm going inside. If you hear shooting and I don't come out, get on the mare and ride like hell."

He pushed open the door of the trading post. The interior was as dark as the narrow windows could make it, and the atmos- phere was rank with the smell of sweat, tobacco, alcohol, and a dozen other odors. After the glare of the afternoon sun the dim light made it difficult for him to see the interior of the store, and he paused by the door to let his eyes adjust.

"What'll you have, stranger?" said a guttural voice out of the dark. Straining to see in the gloom, Starbuck observed that at the far end of the store was a rude bar made from planks laid over some up-ended barrels. Behind the bar Otto Baltz sat on a stool, wiping the sweat from his bare belly with a dirty towel.

Starbuck's eyes were becoming accustomed to the darkness now, and he saw that there were two other men in the room. They were standing at the end of the bar, leaning on the planks with whiskey glasses in their hands. One of the men was tall and thin, the other short and stout; both were roughly dressed and extremely dirty. A nearly-empty whiskey bottle stood before them on the bar, and Starbuck guessed that they were at least a little drunk. Intent on their liquor, they had barely glanced at him when he came through the door.

"Who's riding the buckskin at the hitch rail?" he said.

The tall man swiveled his head around.

"Who wants to know?" he growled.

Baltz stood up, peering at Starbuck in the dim light.

"Say," he said, "I know you. You're the Marshal up at Comanche Wells, ain'tcha?"

The other two men stiffened suddenly.

"Comanche Wells?" said the stout one, startled. He turned to the taller man. "Tim, did he say. . . . "

"Shut up," said the tall man, his eyes fixed on Starbuck. He put down his glass and straightened up, his hands dropping to his sides. Starbuck saw that he was wearing a six-gun butt forward on the right side, Army-style. Ex-soldiers, including deserters, often continued to carry weapons this way out of habit.

The stout man started sidling down the bar away from his companion. He too was carrying a revolver, but Starbuck could see that the holster was badly cut and the weapon old. The stout man might be fast, but he would be the lesser threat; it would be the other man, the tall one, who would draw first, and he would be the faster of the two. Starbuck knew that if there was any gunplay, he would have to take the tall man first, then the stout man . . . if he had time.

"You riding the buckskin?" Starbuck said to the tall man.

"Yeah. So what?"

"You're under arrest."

"The hell you say. What for?"

"Murder, robbery, arson, horse stealing, maybe a rape or two. That do for a start?"

"Wait a minute, Marshal," Baltz said, "you ain't got no jurisdiction here. Leave these men alone."

"I've got all the jurisdiction I need, Baltz," Starbuck snapped, "so shut up. If you interfere again, I'll take you in too."

He glared at the men in front of the bar.

"You two—reach over nice and slow with your left hands and unbuckle those gunbelts."

"Like hell," said the tall man. "There's two of us and only one of you, and you're out of your territory. You ain't got a chance, law dog. We're gonna cut you to pieces."

"Now hold it, men," Baltz cried shrilly. "I run a decent place here, and I don't want no trouble." He was backing hastily into a corner, out of the line of fire.

"There ain't gonna be no trouble," said the tall man. "We're just gonna kill this two-bit tin star here and then have us another drink."

The door behind Starbuck opened suddenly, and Kate Beaumont stood framed in the light. She was holding the double-barreled shotgun, and the hammers were cocked.

"You're not going to kill anybody, you murdering pig," she hissed.

The men at the bar gaped at her.

"What the hell . . . ?" said the stout man.

"Get out of here, Mrs. Beaumont," Starbuck said desperately.

"No," she said, taking a tighter grip on the shotgun.

The tall man's face broke into a broad smile.

"Well, looky here, Porky," he said to the stout man. "Guess we missed something yesterday. Make you a deal . . . whoever downs the law dog gets to take her into the back room first."

"Shut your filthy mouth," Starbuck said.

The tall man laughed, a flat, grating, mirthless sound.

Then he went for his gun.

Starbuck was not taken by surprise, and he was by far the faster of the two. His Colt was in his hand, coming up, as the tall man's six-gun cleared leather. The Colt bucked; dust flew from the front of the tall man's coat and he stumbled back into the bar, overturning the barrels and sending planks, bottles, and glasses crashing to the floor. Starbuck put a second bullet into him to make certain, then whirled toward the other man, who was just raising his pistol to fire. As Starbuck thumbed back the hammer of the Colt for his third shot he saw that it was going to be close—perhaps too close. He had taken too long to dispose of the tall man, and now, if the stout man shot straight. . . .

Then the shotgun bellowed in Starbuck's ear. Kate Beaumont had fired both barrels into the stout man's stomach. Blood and tissue spattered as the man cartwheeled into the wreckage of the bar, twitched once, and lay still.

"Good God!" Baltz gasped. "She killed him!"

"Damned if she didn't," said Starbuck, gazing thoughtfully at her.

He searched the dead men thoroughly, then checked the saddlebags of their horses. As expected, he found money, gold dust, jewelry, and other valuables obviously looted from Comanche Wells. Kate Beaumont watched the proceedings impassively; Starbuck wondered at her apparent calmness after what she had just seen and done.

But at the sight of one item which he found in the dead men's saddlebags, Kate Beaumont nearly broke down. It was a cameo brooch, delicately ornamented with gold filigree. She took it from his hand and stood looking down at it, tears welling up in her eyes.

"What is it?" he asked gently.

"It belonged to my mother," she whispered. "I kept it in a little box in my bedroom. Those men in there . . . they must have been part of the gang that burned our ranch and killed my husband."

"Yes, so it seems."

"But why would those two leave the others and come here?"

"Sometimes after a job some of the gang members will take their cut and go their own way," he said. "Or maybe they were planning to rejoin the rest later. Either way, that's two that won't reach the border. That's all I care about."

He left her and went back inside to take a written statement from Baltz about the shooting. The gunmen had drawn first, but the only living witness that Starbuck and Kate Beaumont had to the shooting was Baltz himself, a known thief and liar and no friend of the law. And Starbuck was, as Baltz had said, out of his jurisdiction. Starbuck feared trouble from the trader over the shooting, but he knew very well what motivated Baltz and men like him. When Baltz learned that Starbuck intended to compensate him handsomely for the damage to his store and pay him a healthy fee for burying the dead men, he signed the statement eagerly. Starbuck slipped the paper into his shirt and counted out the money while Baltz watched, smiling now and mopping his brow with the filthy towel.

When Baltz had accepted the money and pocketed it, Starbuck turned on his heel and started toward the door.

"Come back again, Marshal," Baltz called. "Glad to see you anytime."

Starbuck walked out, slamming the door behind him.

Kate Beaumont was standing beside the horses, staring blankly at the horizon. Her eyes were now dry.

Starbuck shifted his saddle to the buckskin stallion and placed its saddle on the gray mare. When he was finished, he handed the mare's reins to Kate Beaumont.

"I've filled your canteen and there are provisions in the saddlebags, Mrs. Beaumont. As you said this morning, you're now free to go where you please."

"Where are you going, Marshal?"

"South. You?"

She gazed out at the surrounding hills.

"You said that there were at least five men, possibly six, at our ranch?"

"That's my guess."

"So at least three or four of the men who murdered my husband are still alive."

"Yes."

"Then I'm riding with you."

"Now look, Mrs. Beaumont . . ." he began, exasperated.

"Don't worry," she said angrily, "I won't hold you back and I won't get in your way. I can ride as well as any man and shoot as straight as most. I'm going with you, Mr. Starbuck, and you can't stop me."

She put her foot in the stirrup and mounted the mare. Starbuck opened his mouth to protest, and then suddenly changed his mind. The glint in her eyes and the set of her jaw told him that it would be useless to argue with her further. With his permission or without it, the woman was determined to ride after her husband's murderers, and if so it was far better for her— and for his own conscience—that she did not ride alone.

"All right," he said, swinging up onto the buckskin. "Let's get moving."

Starbuck headed southwest, setting a fast pace. He wanted to cut the raiders' trail as quickly as possible. An hour's ride, two at the most, and they should once more pick up the southbound tracks of the stolen horse herd. Kate Beaumont rode doggedly beside him.

It belatedly occurred to Starbuck that she had ignored his urgent warning not to follow him into the trading post.

"I told you back there to stay outside when I went in," he said.

"If I had," she snapped, "you'd probably be dead now."

Startled at the fierceness of her tone, he glanced over at her. Her earlier impassivity had vanished; now her face was deathly pale, and her hands were shaking badly. Starbuck had seen similar reactions in others after a shooting.

"Mrs. Beaumont," he said softly, "have you ever killed anyone before?"

"No," she replied. "Never."

Then she turned in the saddle and stared at him, a strange new light in her eyes.

"Easy, isn't it?" she said.

Starbuck looked away, shaken by the intensity in her voice. He knew that the need for vengeance was twisting both of them into something that they had not previously been, something ugly and terrifying. Yet somehow he didn't care anymore . . . at least not for himself.

They rode on in silence, their anger and grief burning inside them.

CHAPTER FIVE

Two hours out of the trading post they cut across the raiders' trail. Starbuck reined in and dismounted, scrutinizing the ground carefully. The gang was still driving the horse herd due south, and from the tracks he judged that there were still twenty to twenty-five riders, possibly a few more.

At least two of the horses now traveling with the main body had been at the Beaumont ranch the day before, for he recognized the imprint of their hooves.

"The men who killed Tom—the ones who are left, I mean —they've rejoined the rest, then?" said Kate Beaumont when he told her.

"Yes. See that print there? The frog is twisted on that horse's right front shoe. And here—this animal drags its left rear foot just a little. I saw both of those tracks on the ground around your house."

"How far ahead of us are they?"

"A day at least. These prints were made last night, probably before dark."

"You can tell that?"

"Yes. Let's move."

They headed southward, following the tracks of the horse herd and the men who were driving it. At Kate Beaumont's request, he began to explain to her the rudiments of reading sign.

35

"You must be very good at this—tracking, I mean," she said.

"When you track men for a living, you learn fast if you want to stay alive," he replied. "Now I'm rusty. Been a town marshal too long, I guess. Fortunately, a blind man could follow this trail. Later it may get tougher. A lot tougher."

About mid-afternoon they found the first horse. It was lying in the middle of the trail, and as Starbuck reined up beside it he saw that the animal was still alive. It raised its head and whinnied weakly as he approached. Two buzzards which had been waiting expectantly nearby flapped away to a safe distance and then sat patiently, watching him with their beady eyes.

"Broken leg," he said, examining the fallen horse. "Put its foot into that hole there and went down in the middle of the trail. You can see where the rest of the herd divided to go around it. Must have happened yesterday afternoon sometime . . . he's almost done for now."

Starbuck knelt down and gently rubbed the dying animal's neck.

"Nobody even stopped to put it out of its misery," he said sadly.

He drew his Colt. Kate Beaumont looked away.

It was now late afternoon, and as they rode Starbuck felt the tension growing within him. He was fairly certain that the herd and the main body of riders were far ahead of them, but the country was becoming more broken as they approached the border and the marauders had already used the tactic of leaving men behind to discourage pursuit. They might do so again.

"You'd better drop back behind me a little way," he said to Kate Beaumont.

"Why should I?" she flared.

Starbuck sighed.

"Because," he said, "if we ride into an ambush it will be harder for them to get both of us at once if we're spread out a little."

He reined up and faced her.

"Look, Mrs. Beaumont," he said wearily, "you've got to stop getting angry every time I ask you to do something. It has nothing to do with me being male and you being female. Hunting men is my business. I've done it most of my life. I know what we're up against here, you don't."

He gestured at the tracks ahead of them.

"These men we're following are shrewd and absolutely ruthless," he said. "They've been chased before. They'll kill us if they can. And the simple fact is that I haven't got the time or the patience or the wit to fight them and you too. So if you can't play this my way, if you can't do what I ask when I ask it, then turn around and ride north right now. Go home, go anywhere, but let me alone so that I can do what I have to do. All right?"

Kate Beaumont stared at him, biting her lip. Then her body sagged, and he saw that there were tears in her eyes.

"I'm sorry, Mr. Starbuck," she said in a small voice. "It's not you I'm angry at. It's just that . . . I want to see those men die. All of them. I want to be there. I *have* to be there. It's all I can think about. I want to go with you. Please."

Starbuck relented. He couldn't be angry with her, because he knew only too well what she was feeling.

"Tell you what, Mrs. Beaumont," he said. "You can come with me if you stop calling me 'Mr. Starbuck.' My name's Grant."

"I'm Kate," she said. It was the first time that he had ever seen her smile.

"Come on, Kate," he said. "We'll ride together."

As usual, the buzzards warned them first. There were a half-dozen of them, black dots circling lazily in the sky a mile away. Without slowing the pace, Starbuck slid the Winchester out of the scabbard and held it across the saddle. He knew that there was a waterhole ahead, and already he could see that the stolen horses had begun to move faster as they drew nearer to it. The animals had been thirsty and had smelled the water. Perhaps the men driving them had been thirsty too.

As they came down a little slope to the waterhole Starbuck reined in, cursing under his breath. A dead horse lay rotting in the water. It had been shot in the head. Two buzzards were perched on its ribs, tearing at its flesh.

"Why did they kill it there?" Kate Beaumont said.

"To foul the water. It's an old trick to discourage somebody from chasing you through the desert. You dump a body or two into the waterhole—horses, cattle, people, it doesn't matter—and pretty soon the water's unfit to drink. Unless they're carrying a lot of extra water with them, the pursuers have to give up and go back to the previous well or waterhole—if they can make it. If they can't, they die too."

"How horrible."

"I used to think so," he said bleakly, "but after what I've seen in the past two days it seems almost mild by comparison."

They rode on down to the waterhole. Starbuck could tell from the tracks that the horses had been allowed to drink for awhile and had then been driven a little way off to a natural corral formed by a ring of boulders. Spotted about the waterhole were small heaps of ashes where campfires had been built.

"They bedded down here last night," he said, touching one of the burned-out campfires. The ashes were cold. "They didn't even care whether somebody saw the fires. Rested up a few hours, then pushed on."

Kate Beaumont was studying the tracks also.

"When they moved out, they went south again," she said.

"Yes. They're headed for Mexico all right. There's nothing south of here except the Rio Grande, and they'll be across that by tonight if they kept moving all day today."

"Then we can't catch up with them before they cross into Mexico."

"I never expected to after. . . ."

"After you stopped to help me," she said, finishing the thought for him.

"It doesn't matter," he said.

"You'll follow them into Mexico?"

"Lady," said Starbuck, "I'll follow these bastards into Hell if I have to."

A buzzard flopped suddenly up out of a little depression just to the west of the waterhole. Starbuck felt a sudden foreboding. He moved around the edge of the water and started cautiously up the little ridge that blocked his view of the depression. At the top he dropped to the ground and peered over the edge.

The naked body of a woman was staked out in the depression. She had been spreadeagled with her hands and feet tied to wooden pegs driven into the ground. She had been dead for many hours; the corpse had already begun to bloat and blacken in the sun. The buzzards had gotten at her and her eyes were gone. Before they had left her there, her tormenters had cut her throat from ear to ear. Her mouth was stretched wide in a silent, eternal scream.

Starbuck heard a strangled cry behind him; Kate Beaumont had come up behind him and had seen the thing staked out on the ground. She turned away, gagging.

Reluctantly, Starbuck walked down into the hollow and bent over the dead woman. Her features were so distorted that it was hard to be sure, but he was fairly certain that it was . . . had been . . . Marian Granger, one of the women taken from Comanche Wells. He straightened, looking down at her. She and his wife had been good friends.

Kate Beaumont came down the slope of the depression. Her face was white, her eyes sick with horror.

"My God," she whispered. "What kind of animals could do that?"

"No animal would have done it," Starbuck said. "Only men kill for pleasure."

"Can we bury her?"

"We should move on."

"At least cut her loose. Don't leave her there like that."

He nodded.

"All right," he said. "Go on back to the horses."

When she had started to walk back up the slope, he drew a

clasp knife from his pocket and began to cut the rawhide loops that held the corpse's arms and legs to the wooden pegs.

"Grant?" said Kate Beaumont in a low voice.

He looked up to see what she wanted. She was standing at the top of the slope, peering back toward the waterhole. There was something unnaturally stiff about her posture.

"What is it?" he said.

"There's an Indian watching us."

"Where is he?"

"On the other side of the waterhole."

"Just one?"

"That's all I can see."

"Stay there and stay still," he said. "I'm coming."

He walked slowly up to stand beside her, the Winchester draped casually in the crook of his arm. The Indian was sitting calmly on his horse a hundred yards from them, making no attempt to conceal himself. He was wearing a blue coat over buckskin trousers; a single feather was braided into his hair, and a Sharps carbine rested across his thighs.

"It's all right," Starbuck said. "It's John Two Trees. He's one of the Army scouts from Fort Scott."

He walked across to the place where the Indian's pony stood.

"Hello, John," he said. "Long time."

"Long time, Marshal. You catch men yet?"

"Four so far," Starbuck said. "The rest have taken the horses to Mexico. How far back of you is the cavalry?"

"One mile, maybe two. Fort send whole troop."

Starbuck looked to the north and saw the rising clouds of dust that marked the cavalry's approach.

"About time," he said bitterly.

The soldiers came up slowly in a column of twos, accompanied by the usual symphony of creaking leather and jingling metal. Starbuck was relieved to see that Sam Lattimer was in command. Lattimer had been a captain ever since his orders brought him west after the War; he had grown gray in the service of his country with little thanks and no promotion, but Starbuck knew him to be a good soldier, wise in the ways of the land and a man of unquestioned courage.

Lattimer brought the column to a halt a few yards from where they were standing and gave the orders to dismount. The troopers got down stiffly from their horses, dusty and solemn; there was none of the banter usually exchanged among soldiers at the end of a hard ride. It was apparent that they were very tired.

Lattimer waited until his men had all dismounted, then got down himself and came over to shake Starbuck's hand. Together they walked down toward the waterhole.

"Good to see you, Grant," said Lattimer. "Frank Hardesty brought the word to the Fort, and we got moving as quickly as we could. Damned Army never does anything in a hurry, as you know. We came through Comanche Wells to pick up the trail. Left some supply wagons and a doctor there. I didn't stop to sightsee, but it looked pretty bad. Your family okay?"

"They're dead."

Lattimer swore.

"I'm sorry, son. God, I'm sorry. Glad to see you're all right, though. To tell the truth, I figured you'd be dead too . . . I mean. . . ."

"I was out trailing some rustled steers when they hit," said Starbuck. "Got back too late to do anything."

"We found some dead people along the trail," Lattimer said. "Two of the women hostages, raped and murdered." He shook his head. "This is a rough bunch we're chasing. There were a couple of men too, what was left of them, up by the twin buttes. You do that?"

"Yeah, they were left behind as a rear guard. I got by them all right, but further on about a half-dozen of the gang broke off from the main body and raided the Beaumont ranch above Indian Springs. Killed Beaumont and rode on. I guess you already know about that. I ran into two of them at Indian Springs earlier today. Wasn't trailing them, just came across them by accident. I was taking Mrs. Beaumont over there to get her a horse."

"Don't see any prisoners with you. They shoot it out?"

"Yeah. I got one, Mrs. Beaumont got the other. With a shotgun."

Lattimer whistled and looked back to where Kate Beaumont was standing, watching them.

"Must be some woman," he said.

"Stubborn as a mule," said Starbuck. "Knows how to shoot, though—fortunately for me."

Lattimer sent a detail to drag the dead horse out of the waterhole and another to bury Mrs. Granger. A sergeant came back to report completion of the task. He looked slightly ill.

"You okay, O'Brien?" Lattimer asked, seeing the sergeant's pale face.

"I'm okay, sir. It's just that we're gettin' tired of seein' what those scum are doin' to the women they took. Been in the Army sixteen years and never saw nothin' like this."

He saluted and started to move away, then paused and came back.

"We gonna keep movin', sir?"

Lattimer glanced at the sun, which was now touching the western horizon.

"No. We'll rest here for a couple of hours."

Starbuck started to protest, but Sergeant O'Brien spoke first.

"With respect, Cap'n," O'Brien said, "most of the men would like to go on, sir. They want to catch up with those people before they get across the river."

"I know, Sergeant," Lattimer said, "but in the first place they're probably over the border already, and even if they're not we can't risk blundering into them in the pitch dark. There'll be a half-moon tonight, should be up about ten o'clock. We'll give the horses and the men a break and get something to eat, then start out again at moonrise."

"Yessir," said O'Brien.

"Tell Lieutenant Finley to put out double the usual number

of sentries. The rest of the men may sleep, but no stacked arms. Each man keeps his carbine beside him."

The sergeant saluted again and departed.

"Sorry about the delay, Grant," Lattimer said. "I want to catch up with those people as much as you do, but I'm not going to risk riding into an ambush in the dark with dead-tired horses and nearly as many men shooting at me as I've got to shoot back with."

"That's all right," said Starbuck. "I understand." He looked to the south, where the last rays of the sunset were now touching the highest hills. He didn't have to wait; he could ride on and let the Army follow in its own good time.

"You can go on now if you want to, of course," said Lattimer, as if reading his thoughts, "but I'd suggest you wait here and move out with us later, when the moon is up and we have some light. Otherwise we might come up behind you in the dark and wind up trading shots with you, thinking you were one of the raiders."

He gave Starbuck's arm a fatherly pat.

"You look dead tired, anyway," he said. "A little sleep wouldn't hurt you. Tired men make mistakes, Grant, and at odds of thirty to one, mistakes are something you can't afford right now."

Starbuck hesitated. He wanted to go on, but he had been without sleep for over thirty-six hours and under intense emotional strain for most of that, and he knew that he should rest. Still. . . .

Kate Beaumont walked up, and he introduced her to Lattimer. She shook hands with the officer, and then smiled wanly at Starbuck.

"Are we riding on, Grant?" she said.

Even in the dwindling light he could see that she was in the last stages of exhaustion. Starbuck was prepared to drive himself, but he was not prepared to do it to Kate Beaumont.

"We'll rest a bit," he said. "The soldiers will be moving out in a couple of hours. We'll wait for them."

Lattimer cleared his throat self-consciously.

"Ah, about that, Mrs. Beaumont . . . ," he said. "When we resume the march tonight I'll leave a detachment of soldiers here with you. You can get some rest and the troopers will escort you back to the Fort in the morning. After that you can. . . ."

"Thank you, Captain, but I'm going with you."

Lattimer frowned.

"I'm sorry," he said, "but I can't permit it. If we catch up to this bunch there'll be fighting, lots of it, and some people are going to get hurt. I can't endanger your life by allowing you to accompany us."

"I'm going with you, Captain."

"No, ma'am, you're not. You're a civilian, Mrs. Beaumont, and the Army's standing orders prohibit civilians from accompanying troops in the field."

"Marshal Starbuck is a civilian."

"Marshal Starbuck is a sworn law officer. You're not."

"Please, Captain," she said. There was a note of desperation in her voice. "Those men butchered my husband and destroyed my home. I have a right to be there, to see them punished. Please let me come."

Lattimer shook his head. When he spoke there was genuine regret in his voice.

"I can't, Mrs. Beaumont," he said. "It's not personal, believe me. I know that you can take care of yourself—the Marshal told me what you did at Indian Springs. But within a few hours we may be engaged in a pitched battle with this gang of killers, and there's no guarantee that we'll win. These men are tough and hard, and they have almost as many men as we do. They might wipe out this entire troop—it's happened before. Then what would become of you? You've seen what they've done to other women. I don't want that to happen to you. I won't *let* it happen. Please try to understand."

"I appreciate your concern, Captain," she said, "but it's my life, and my choice. I choose to go with you."

Starbuck raised an eyebrow at Lattimer.

"Told you she was stubborn," he said.

44

CHAPTER SIX

But Captain Lattimer was stubborn too, and when the troop finally mounted up to resume the chase Kate Beaumont was left behind. Lattimer detailed a lieutenant and four men to remain with her. He gave the lieutenant emphatic orders not to let her near her horse until the detachment started north for the Fort at daylight.

Starbuck saddled up, then led the buckskin over to the little knoll where Kate Beaumont was sitting disconsolately watching the troop prepare to move out. The light of the rising half-moon clearly revealed the fatigue and sadness in her face.

"I'm sorry, Kate," he said, stopping beside her. "I tried to explain to Lattimer how you feel, but he's made up his mind. Don't think too harshly of him. He's seen those other women, just as you and I have, and he doesn't want you to end up that way too."

"I know," she said in a tired voice. "Thank you for trying, Grant. Thank you for everything."

The young lieutenant whom Lattimer had left in charge of Kate's escort approached them.

"The men have a pot of coffee over there by the fire, Mrs. Beaumont, if you'd care for some," he said. "We'll saddle up and head north at daylight."

"Thank you, Lieutenant. I'll be over directly."

The lieutenant touched his hat to her and walked away.

"The soldiers will get you to Fort Scott," said Starbuck. "What will you do then?"

She stood up, brushing the dirt from her clothing.

"I don't know," she said. "Perhaps I'll just wait there at the Fort until I hear . . . what happens."

Starbuck stepped up into the saddle.

"Take care of yourself, Kate," he said.

"You too," she replied, a little wistfully.

Lattimer was bawling orders to his men, and presently the clamor of leather and metal began again as the troop formed its column of twos and began to move out. Starbuck wheeled the buckskin and started after them. When he reached the top of the rise he twisted in the saddle and looked back. She was still standing there, looking small and forlorn in the moonlight.

As he turned to follow the soldiers she raised her hand to him in farewell.

The cavalry moved south at a rapid pace. Riding to the front of the column, Starbuck studied the troopers as he passed them. He noted with approval that there was no conversation and no inattention among the soldiers as they rode; these men were veterans—tough, serious, and professional. No doubt they realized the truth of what their commander had said earlier . . . that if they did corner the small army of killers they were trailing, there would be a hard fight with no quarter asked or given, and no guarantee of the outcome. Many of these men might well be dead before the next sunset.

He fell in beside Captain Lattimer and they rode silently forward, feeling the tension growing around them. Lattimer had the troop moving at a fast trot, a gait which was easy on the horses but which ate up the miles rapidly. The hoofprints of their quarry were plainly visible in the half-light. Somewhere up ahead John Two Trees and the other scouts were following the same trail, watching for any sign of an ambush.

"I make it about eight or nine hours to the border," Lattimer said. "If they're still on this side of the river, we should be in contact during the early morning."

"If they're still on this side of the river, they're either very brave or very stupid," Starbuck said. "They should be well into Mexico by now."

"I'll bet on stupid," Lattimer muttered. "Or maybe it's just plain arrogance. So far they've moved very slowly, almost as if they don't care whether they're being chased or not. The scouts say they didn't break camp at the waterhole until after daylight this morning. Sat around there the whole damn night, when they should have been high-tailing for Mexico."

"Whiskey bottles all over the place back there," said Starbuck. "Started their celebration a little early, maybe. Had to sober up before they could move on."

"Maybe," said Lattimer. "And they had the women."

Starbuck felt sickened by the thought of what that long night must have been like for the hostages from Comanche Wells. For one it had brought a hideous death. But perhaps her torment had bought precious time for the pursuers.

"Sam," he said, "we've got to catch these people. Some of the women may still be alive. They took seven, and we've only found three of them."

"Don't hope for too much there, son," Lattimer said. "I've been in this country for almost twenty years, and I wish I could tell you how many times I've ridden after Indians or white renegades or Mexican bandits who hit towns and ranches and took women away with them. Getting them back is chancy at best. Usually if the cavalry gets too close to the raiders they kill their hostages. So even if we do catch up with this bunch, don't count on seeing those women alive again."

An hour before sunrise they rested the horses for fifteen minutes, then mounted up and rode on, still at the trot. Soon the dawn began to streak the eastern sky, and the shadowy hills and rocks and cactus through which they were passing began to take firmer shape in the first light of the new day. Sergeant O'Brien, exercising his privileged position as the troop's top soldier, moved up beside Lattimer.

"Horses are getting pretty tired, Cap'n," he said.

"So am I, Sergeant, so am I. But I can stand it if you can."

"I reckon we'll make it, sir."

"Damn right we will."

The sun was above the eastern horizon when a horseman materialized out of the rocks, hand raised in salute. It was John Two Trees.

"Much shooting ahead," he said. "Scouts hear."

"How far ahead?" said Lattimer.

"Maybe two, three miles."

"How far to the Rio Grande now?"

"Maybe two, three miles."

"Damn," said Lattimer. "Some kind of fight at the river. What would that be all about? We'd better go find out."

He shouted an order, and the column broke into a canter.

Within a few minutes they heard it too—sporadic gunfire close ahead. A half-mile in front of them the trail led over a rise and down between two steep rock walls.

"River there," said John Two Trees, pointing.

Lattimer shouted more orders; as one man the troopers drew their Sharps carbines from their saddle scabbards and loaded them, then rode with them held against their thighs.

"Sergeant O'Brien!" Lattimer bellowed.

"Sir!"

"I'm going to halt the troop below the crest of the hill. The Rio Grande is just beyond. I'll ride forward and see what's what before we go barging down that slope."

"Yessir!"

Another scout rode back from the rocks above the river and said something to John Two Trees.

"Men fight on other side of river," Two Trees announced.

"How many?"

"Many. Hard to see. Much smoke. Some men hide in rocks, other men shoot at them."

The troop halted just below the crest and Lattimer rode forward, Starbuck right beside him. They cantered up the hill and reined in their horses at the top.

Below them the Rio Grande—called by the Mexicans the Rio Bravo—wound between the cliffs, wide and shallow, dividing the two countries. A third of a mile away across the river a gunfight was in progress on the Mexican side. The smaller group, consisting of perhaps six or eight men, was fighting dismounted from the shelter of the rocks near the base of the cliffs, while a dozen men or more on horseback were circling them, firing into the rocks as they rode.

Lattimer put his binoculars to his eyes, steadying his horse so that he could get a better view. Then he swore loudly.

"What's going on?" Starbuck said, trying to control the buckskin stallion which was reacting nervously to the gunfire.

"Detachment of Mexican regulars," said Lattimer. "Maybe a border guard detail—the Mexican army patrols these river crossings sometimes. Somebody's got them outnumbered and pinned in those rocks. Looks like casualties on both sides."

He handed Starbuck the binoculars. With their aid he could make out several figures in Mexican army uniforms among the boulders, and a motley collection of rough-looking men circling them on horseback. Two dead horses and several human bodies were lying on the ground not far from the boulders.

"Those are Mexican regulars in the rocks, all right," Starbuck said.

"What about the others? They look like bandits right enough. Think they're some of the lads we're chasing?"

"Not sure," said Starbuck. "But that white horse lying dead there just west of the rocks . . . it's got a black splash on its rump that seems familiar to me. Could be one of the horses taken from Comanche Wells."

He handed back the binoculars.

"Whoever they are," said Lattimer, "they've got those Mexican troopers outnumbered and they're getting ready to wipe them out. Look—they're bunching up to charge in and finish them off."

Even without the binoculars, Starbuck could see the attackers gathering their forces for a final assault on the Mexicans.

"What are you going to do, Sam?" he said.

"Well," said Lattimer morosely, "I'm not about to sit here and watch that bunch of bandits wipe out those soldiers."

He twisted in his saddle.

"Sergeant O'Brien!" he shouted. "Bring up the troop!"

"Sir!"

The cavalrymen moved quickly up behind Lattimer and Starbuck. Lattimer waved them forward and spurred his horse down the slope onto the broad bank of the river; the troop followed him, still in column.

Lattimer drew his saber.

"Ever see a cavalry charge, Grant?" he said, grinning broadly.

Starbuck stared at him.

"You're going to cross the river?" he said. "I thought the Army had orders not to go across to the Mexican side. If I remember right, the last officer who took U.S. troops into Mexico got himself court-martialed."

"So I've heard. You coming?"

Starbuck slid the Winchester out of the scabbard and jacked a shell into the chamber.

"Sam," he said, "it's no damned wonder you're still a captain. What are we waiting for?"

Lattimer wheeled his horse.

"D Troop!" he called. "Form column of fours! Smartly now!"

The troopers moved quickly and smoothly into a formation four riders abreast.

"All right," Lattimer shouted, "we're going across to assist those Mexican Army troopers. When we hit the Mexican shore, move out into line abreast and go like hell! Ready, Grant?"

"Let 'er buck."

Lattimer raised his sword and pointed it toward the distant shore.

"Troop forward," he roared. "At the gallop! Bugler, sound the charge! *Charge!*"

The bugler clapped the bugle to his lips and the clear, pealing notes of the charge echoed against the walls of the surrounding cliffs. Instantly the troop's excited horses leaped forward, reaching the gallop within a few jumps as they followed their captain headlong down the bank and into the waters of the Rio Grande.

The buckskin reared at the sudden explosion of sound and action, almost unseating Starbuck; then the stallion stretched out its neck and charged furiously after the rest. They all plunged together into the shallow water, sending sheets of spray flying high above the riders' heads. The troopers were yelling wildly, egged on by the insistent clamor of the bugle. Somewhere in the din some unregenerate Confederate was giving a Rebel Yell.

Within a hundred yards the buckskin had pulled abreast of Lattimer at the head of the troop. Without any urging from Starbuck the stallion forged ahead, pulling away from the cavalrymen as they stormed through the river.

"Damn it, Grant," Lattimer roared, "wait for me!"

But Starbuck was in no mood to wait, nor could he have checked the stallion even if he had wanted to. The animal's blood was up, and so was Starbuck's. The bugle call, the shouts, the thunder of the pounding hooves, and the sheer, raw power of the charging wall of horseflesh and armed men—it was beyond anything in his experience. He found himself suddenly a man gone berserk, not thinking but only feeling, overwhelmed by a fighting madness born of the exhilaration of the charge and the emotions which it evoked. Grief, anger, frustration, bitterness, desire for revenge—all boiled up in him in one primal, animal rage as he drove the straining stallion at the opposite shore.

Suddenly he was out of the river, racing up the sand on the Mexican side. He saw that the sound of the bugle and the headlong approach of the cavalry troop had thrown the bandits into complete disarray; their horses reared and bucked as their riders wheeled and fled away from the river, the Mexican soldiers in the rocks forgotten.

Starbuck was firing now, the flat crack of the Winchester almost lost in the deeper roar of the cavalrymen's Sharps carbines. One of the fleeing bandits went down as his horse cartwheeled over him; another tumbled out of the saddle as a heavy Sharps bullet raised a sudden cloud of dust on the back of his coat. Then a third rider threw up his arms and fell backwards over his horse's rump; the two horsemen immediately behind him trampled over him without pausing in their flight.

One of the bandits came angling across in front of Starbuck from the left; the man saw him and raised his pistol at almost point-blank range. Starbuck shot him off the horse. The riderless animal crashed into the buckskin, and both horses went down squealing and kicking. Starbuck twisted clear of the falling buckskin and landed heavily on his back, losing the Winchester. Quickly he scrambled to his feet, trying to see through the dust clouds stirred up by the mêlée.

He looked around for the Winchester and saw it on the ground twenty feet from him. As he ran for it, another horseman charged at him out of the curtain of dust. The rider was a thin man in a huge sombrero, wearing two bandoliers crossed over his chest. He fired his pistol at Starbuck; the bullet plucked at Starbuck's shirt, missing his ribs by a fraction of an inch. Starbuck drew his Colt and fired twice, knocking the man to the ground. Despite the fall and the two slugs in his body, the man raised himself up to fire again. Starbuck's third shot knocked him back to the earth, dead.

Still holding the Colt, Starbuck scooped up the Winchester with his left hand and peered around, but there were no other riders near him. As the dust settled he saw the last of the bandits disappearing into a canyon to the south, leaving a trail of downed horses and dead and wounded men behind them.

The bugle sounded again, and Starbuck recognized the staccato notes of the recall. A dozen troopers came riding reluctantly back toward the river, holstering their carbines as they formed up near the bank.

The buckskin had struggled to its feet, apparently unharmed.

Starbuck caught the animal, remounted, and rode back to join the troopers.

Lattimer was there beside his hard-breathing horse, still holding his saber. The blade was bloody, and he wiped it before sliding it back into its scabbard. As Starbuck dismounted, Lattimer grinned at him.

"Well," he said, "what did you think of it?"

Starbuck could only shake his head in wonder. His breathing was still rapid, his pulse still racing. Only now was the wild exhilaration, the fighting madness of the charge beginning to fade.

"You boys do this kind of thing often, Sam?" he said.

"You know," Lattimer replied, "in twenty-two years in the Army I've only been in three all-out cavalry charges. Hell of a feeling, isn't it?"

"Beats tequila anytime," Starbuck said wryly. He glanced over Lattimer's shoulder. A Mexican officer was approaching.

"Here comes your opposite number, Sam."

The officer saluted Lattimer gravely and introduced himself.

"Teniente Roberto Alejandro Guerrero y Vega at your service, Capitán," he said politely.

Lattimer returned the salute. "I'm Lattimer, D Troop, out of Fort Scott," he said, "and this is Marshal Grant Starbuck."

"I am deeply grateful to you gentlemen for your assistance," said Lieutenant Guerrero. "Another minute or two and it would have been the end for us. Those accursed bandidos would have cut us to ribbons if you had not arrived when you did."

"It was a pleasure, Teniente," Lattimer replied. "But I see that some of your men are wounded, as are some of mine. I don't have a doctor with me, but we have medical supplies. May I share them with you?"

"Again, Capitán, my thanks. It is most gracious of you."

"Then if you'll excuse me, I'll see to my men." He hurried away, shouting for Sergeant O'Brien.

Guerrero smiled pleasantly at Starbuck.

"May I inquire, Marshal, how we happened to have the good fortune to find you and Capitán Lattimer's men in this vicinity?"

Starbuck told him of the raid on Comanche Wells and what had occurred since. When he spoke of the butchered women, the Mexican officer flushed with anger.

"Filthy animals," he said. "It shames me that such men use my country as a hiding place from which to commit their atrocities."

"Only a few of them were Mexicans, Teniente," Starbuck said. "Most of them were Americans—Norteamericanos, as you say. The shame is that such men exist in any country, and that it's so difficult for men like you and me to catch and destroy them."

Slowly matters on the riverbank were brought to a semblance of order. The dead and wounded were counted: Lieutenant Guerrero had lost two men killed and three of his soldiers had been wounded, leaving only five fit for duty. Lattimer's cavalry had suffered no fatalities but six men had received wounds, most of them minor. Of the bandits, six were dead; one wounded man was found, but he died where he lay before he could be questioned. Seven horses had been killed or were hurt so badly that they had to be destroyed.

When the wounded had been cared for and the dead men and horses buried, Lattimer rejoined Starbuck and Guerrero.

"A heavy butcher's bill, Teniente," he said. "I only wish that we had accounted for more of them, but that long ride through the water slowed us down and gave them a good jump on us. But at least we prevented them from doing further harm to you and your men."

Guerrero nodded.

"It may be that we have both had a fortunate escape this morning, Capitán," he said. "I think that those bandidos were lying in wait for you last night on the Estados Unidos side of the river. When my patrol arrived here yesterday evening we saw the tracks of the horse herd coming out of the water and heading off into the canyons to the south. Since we had no knowledge at that time that the horses were stolen we did not pursue them, but made camp here in the rocks last night. It was at dawn that we saw these other men coming across the river. I think that perhaps they had been left behind by the others to ambush you, but grew tired of waiting and decided to follow their compadres into Mexico. When we saw them crossing we challenged them, they attacked us, and the rest you know."

"Your hunch about the ambush is correct, Teniente," said Lattimer. "Our scouts found signs that at least a dozen men were waiting in the rimrock over there on the U.S. side for most of the night, watching their back trail. If we had come up to them in the dark, they would have slaughtered us."

He gave Starbuck a thin smile.

"Sometimes it pays to be late," he said.

"What now, Sam?" Starbuck asked.

"Well," said Lattimer, "that may be up to the Lieutenant here. Teniente, as you well know, U.S. Army troops are not allowed to cross the Rio Grande without the permission of the Mexican government. I took a great liberty in riding across this morning, and I can only hope that under the circumstances you were not too distressed by my action."

"On the contrary, Capitán," said Guerrero with a smile, "I am quite pleased by it, since otherwise I would very probably be dead right now. We shall consider that my permission was given, and say no more of the matter."

"The remaining question," said Lattimer, "is whether we may now pursue these murdering vultures and catch them before they escape into the badlands to the south. My government says that I may not lead U.S. troops into Mexico on my own authority, but I'd like to suggest that I place myself and my men under your command, so that we're acting under your orders. Then we can all give chase together."

"Alas," Guerrero said, raising his hands in a gesture of frustration, "I cannot accept your generous offer. My government, like yours, has a very strict policy in such matters. If you were to attempt to proceed into Mexico now, I would be required to oppose you—by force of arms, if necessary. A futile gesture, of course, since you could easily dispose of us, but it would be my duty to try to stop you nevertheless. In view of what you have just done for me and for my men, it would sadden me greatly to find myself in such a position."

"I understand, Teniente," said Lattimer. "I compliment you upon both your courage and your devotion to your duty. No confrontation will be necessary. I've made my offer; since you can't accept it, my troop will now recross the river and return to our post at Fort Scott."

He grimaced at Starbuck.

"Sorry, Grant," he said. "You heard the lieutenant. He can't give us his permission and I can't go on without it. International politics at their worst. I've already put my head on the block by crossing that damned river, and unless I get the troop back on the U.S. side pronto, I'll be retiring from the Army next week as a private. Damn all politicians, anyway," he muttered, slapping his gloves hard against his leg in disgust.

Sergeant O'Brien was standing a few steps away, listening.

"Sir," he said, "the men ain't goin' to like turnin' back. They want to go after those sidewinders. All you gotta do is say the word, Cap'n. We'll follow you."

"I appreciate that, Sergeant," said Lattimer, "but you know the regulations as well as I do. Besides, you heard the Teniente. We'd have to fight him first."

"Well," said O'Brien, eyeing Guerrero speculatively, "no disrespect to the Teniente or his men, sir, but there's only five or six of 'em. . . ."

"I know, Sergeant," Lattimer said, "but we have our orders, and in any case I don't want to be remembered as the man who started another war with Mexico. Now get the troop ready to start back across the river."

"Okay, Cap'n. Wish there was some other way, though."

Lattimer turned back to Starbuck.

"God knows I'd like to go after them, son," he said. "You heard O'Brien—we all would. But we can't. You know we can't."

"I know, Sam. It's all right. I expected it. It took a lot of guts just to bring your people this far. Please thank your men for their offer."

"What about you?" Lattimer said. "You can do as you please, of course, but if you're smart you'll come back with us."

"Teniente," said Starbuck to Lieutenant Guerrero, "will you and your men be going after the bandits?"

"I regret not, señor. My instructions are to patrol the border crossings. I am not allowed to pursue bandidos into the interior. And, like Capitán Lattimer, I must obey my orders."

"Do you have any objections if I go after them?"

Guerrero gaped at him. "Alone, señor? There are too many. There are still twenty, perhaps twenty-five of them. You will be killed."

"Teniente," Starbuck said, "are you married?"

"But of course," said Guerrero, perplexed. "I have a wife and three lovely daughters in Chihuahua."

"Well, Teniente, those lice we're trailing left my wife and my two small sons burned to death in the ashes of my house in Comanche Wells. If you can picture your wife and children dead in the ruins of your own home then perhaps you'll understand how I feel."

He picked up the buckskin's reins.

"I'm going to get every one of the men who did that, Teniente," he said. "Every one of them. If you try to stop me from following them from here, I'll just go back across the river, then go upstream or downstream a few miles and cross back over. Whatever it takes, however long it takes, I'm going to find them, with your help or without it. I hope that what I have just said hasn't offended you, but that's how I feel, and that's what I'm going to do."

"I am not offended, señor," Guerrero replied. "I am deeply sorry about your family, and I wish that I could help. You are free to ride where you please in my country. I only regret that you must go alone."

"I don't think he's going to be alone," said Lattimer. "Not quite, anyway."

Puzzled, Starbuck turned; Lattimer was staring back at the river. Starbuck followed his gaze and saw a solitary rider entering the water on the American side and splashing toward them through the shallows. Long before she reached the Mexican shore, Starbuck could see that the rider was Kate Beaumont.

"Good morning, Marshal," she said, reining in beside them. "Good morning, Captain Lattimer."

"Teniente," said Starbuck, "this is Mrs. Beaumont. Her husband was killed by the bandits. Mrs. Beaumont, Lieutenant Guerrero, of the Mexican Army."

Guerrero bowed.

"I am honored, señora," he said, eyeing her with approval.

Lattimer took off his hat and wiped his face with his neckerchief.

"Mrs. Beaumont," he said with a trace of irony, "what have you done with Lieutenant Finley and his men?"

"Please don't blame the Lieutenant," she said. "He's a very nice boy, and I'm sorry for any embarrassment I may have caused him. I led him to believe that I was sleeping soundly, and was able to slip away before he discovered otherwise. He's just over the hill on the other side of the river, riding as hard as he can trying catch up with me. Please give him my apologies."

She dismounted and stood beside them, glancing around at the traces of the battle.

"I take it that they got away?" she said.

"Not all of them," said Lattimer. "We killed seven. Your friend the Marshal here got two himself. But, yes, most of them got away. I'm sorry."

"And now you're turning back."

"I have no choice. This is Mexico. I have no authority here. I'm truly sorry."

She looked at Starbuck.

"Grant, you're going after them, aren't you?"

"Of course."

"Good. So am I."

Starbuck shook his head.

"Kate, you can't. Things are different now. We're in Mexico. We won't have the Army with us. We'll be all alone. You don't know what it's like out there in the badlands. Please, let's not go through this again."

"I'm going, Grant. You know I'm going."

"Sam," said Starbuck in desperation, "will you please tie her to that horse and take her back with you?"

"He can't," said Kate Beaumont. "He has no authority on this side of the river. He just said so."

"Kate. . . ."

"I think I've heard this part before," said Lattimer, pulling on his gloves. "Sergeant O'Brien, is the troop ready to move?"

"Yessir. Wounded have already been taken to the U.S. side of the river."

"Very well, Sergeant." Lattimer climbed into the saddle. "D Troop!" he shouted. "Prepare to mount! Mount!"

He reached down to shake hands with Guerrero and Starbuck.

"Good luck, son," he said to Starbuck. "God be with you."

"Thank you, Sam."

"Mrs. Beaumont," said Lattimer, "you are a very exasperating woman, and a very brave one. I wish you well also."

He saluted her, then lifted his arm and waved the troop forward. They splashed slowly across the river toward the American shore and began the climb up the far slope. Soon the end of the column had passed from sight over the crest of the hill.

Kate Beaumont gazed defiantly at Starbuck.

"Well?" she demanded.

He regarded her thoughtfully. Two days ago, he and this woman had been total strangers, victims of similar but separate tragedies with nothing in common except their grief. Now their lives were bound together by circumstance; they shared a savage obsession, and seemed destined to share a savage trail as well.

"I hope you've still got that shotgun," he said grimly. "We may need it."

CHAPTER SEVEN

Starbuck and Kate Beaumont watered their horses and filled their canteens at the river, then walked back to where Lieutenant Guerrero was forming up the tattered remains of his command.

"Teniente," Starbuck said, "it's been an honor to meet you. Now, with your permission, Mrs. Beaumont and I will be on our way."

Guerrero's expression was grave.

"You are both very courageous people," he said. "It is most unfortunate that my orders make it impossible for me to ride with you. However, I have been thinking, and I believe that there is at least one small thing that I can do for you, if you will permit me. Fernández!"

A burly Mexican sergeant stepped forward.

"Señor, Señora, this is Sergeant Diego Fernández. He has been with me for many years. He was, in fact, one of my father's vaqueros when I was a boy, and has remained with me ever since I joined the Army. He is a man of many talents and great courage. Do you speak Spanish, Marshal?"

"Yes, Teniente," said Starbuck. "I was raised in the border country. Mrs. Beaumont knows your language also."

"Excellent," said Guerrero. "Fernández speaks English reasonably well, but his abilities lie mainly in other directions. His mother was a Yaqui Indian, and he has many skills which may mean the difference between life and death in the country into which you will be riding."

He addressed the Sergeant in a soft, firm voice.

"Fernández," he said, "you will accompany the Marshal and the Señora wherever they wish to go. You will assist them in any way that you can, and you will defend their lives with your own, exactly as you would do for me. It is my wish, and my command. Do you understand?"

"Yes, Teniente."

"Good. Do not fail me. Now go and bring up your horse. Marshal, I assume that you wish to leave immediately?"

"Yes, Lieutenant. Thank you. This is a great kindness. I will try to see that your sergeant returns safely to you."

"I would be glad of that, since it will mean that you are returning safely also. If you should find that there is anything further that I can do for you, my men and I are garrisoned at the Presidio at Rio Del Norte. Do you know it?"

"Yes," said Starbuck.

"Good. You can usually get word to me there. And now I too must go. I have to rendezvous this evening with another patrol at the next crossing upriver. Go with God, my friends, until we meet again."

Guerrero and his remaining soldiers mounted their horses and filed off along the river, heading westward. Starbuck, Kate Beaumont, and Sergeant Fernández stood alone by the banks of the Rio Bravo.

Starbuck examined Fernández with a keen eye. The man was big, well over six feet, and his shoulders and arms bulged beneath the uniform shirt. His face was calm and intelligent, and his eyes met Starbuck's without wavering. His bearing was respectful but not obsequious; his smile was friendly. He had the air of a man who laughed often and enjoyed life. Starbuck, like most men in the west, had of necessity learned to judge men quickly and accurately. For a lawman this ability was essential to continued survival, and it had stood Starbuck in good stead more than once. He decided that he liked what he saw of Fernández.

"Sergeant," he said, "you understand about the men we are chasing? You understand what they have done?"

"Yes, Señor. The Teniente has told me about your town and the murder of your family and all the others. Those men are devils, and they deserve to die. I will enjoy helping you kill them."

"They have us badly outnumbered," said Starbuck, watching him for any sign of fear. "This may be a one-way trip."

"I am not afraid to die," said Fernández calmly.

"Death is the least of it, Sergeant. Do you know what these people will do to us—and the Señora—if we fall into their hands?"

"Yes, Señor. But the answer to that is very simple. We must see that they fall into our hands instead."

Starbuck grinned at him.

"Let's ride," he said.

Soon after they left the river, the trail began to wind through the rough and spectacular terrain which characterizes the country south of the Rio Grande. Great pinnacles of rock rose around them, and deep chasms opened up before and beside them. It was a dry, barren, desolate, cruelly beautiful country; at times it seemed that the three of them might as well have been riding through the mountains of the moon. And though it was beautiful, it was also a fierce, hard land, a land never tamed by anyone—not by the Spaniards, nor by the French during their occupation of Mexico, nor by the Mexicans themselves. It was said, and truthfully so, that tribes of Indians lived deep in these inaccessible wastes who were fiercer even than the dreaded Apaches, warriors who lived as their ancestors had lived for centuries, who had never seen white men . . . or who killed them on sight if they did. Starbuck had also heard that far back in those primeval mountains were canyons wider and deeper even than the Grand Canyon of the Colorado River, but those were only rumors. Few Americans had ever ventured into that country, much less come out again.

But the wild beauty of the land was wasted upon Starbuck and Kate Beaumont; their thoughts were of men, not mountains. Both Starbuck and Fernández rode with their rifles across their saddles, and all of them watched the trail and the rocks ahead with equal care, for they knew that another ambush was all too likely.

For a time it was easy to follow the trail of their quarry; the ground was sandy, and the sand showed the tracks plainly. It was even easy to distinguish the prints of the slowly-moving main body from those of the men who had fled at a gallop from the gunfight at the river that morning. Their tracks indicated that they were moving rapidly to catch up with their companions.

Soon, however, the ground became harder, with long stretches of solid rock beneath the horses' hooves. At times, Starbuck found himself sorely put to follow the trail at all. Had not some of the horses that they were following been shod, he would have been at a loss. As it was, once or twice he had to stop and cast around for a moment to make certain of the right direction to take. Here the first of Fernández' talents was displayed; each time Starbuck became uncertain, with the greatest of tact the Sergeant pointed out some minute mark on the rock which had escaped his notice. Finally he put Fernández in the lead and let him do the tracking while he himself watched for trouble in the rocks ahead.

For the most part they rode single file, but when the trail broadened for a time and the threat of ambush was momentarily lessened, Starbuck dropped back to ride beside Kate Beaumont.

"You've probably gotten that poor lieutenant—Finley—cashiered for letting you get away from him," he said.

"I couldn't go back," she said. "I just couldn't. I had to follow you. When I heard all the shooting, I was afraid that I was too late, that I wouldn't be there at the finish. And I was afraid that you'd be killed in the fighting."

"Would you have cared?" said Starbuck, surprised.

"Of course I would have cared. I . . . I owe you a great deal. I wouldn't like to see you hurt. Besides, I knew that the Army wouldn't go on, and that if you were killed or badly hurt that would be the end of it. The men who killed my husband would escape into Mexico and no one would ever catch them."

She patted her horse's neck.

"I nearly foundered this poor mare getting to the river to see what had happened. I'm sorry those men got away, but I'm happy that you're all right."

Starbuck said nothing for awhile, then spoke up.

"I'm glad you came, Kate," he said.

She smiled shyly at him.

"You told Captain Lattimer you wanted me to go back."

"I lied," he said.

She laughed. It was a good laugh, the first that he had ever heard from her.

"Just one thing, Kate," he said, serious again.

"Yes?"

"Whatever happens, save one bullet for yourself. Do you understand me? Don't let these men take you alive."

"I'd rather save the bullet for one of them."

"You've got to promise me, Kate."

"Don't worry about me, Grant."

"I'm not worried about you," he said brutally. "I'm worried about me. I don't want to die listening to your screams."

The shock showed in Kate Beaumont's face.

"All right," she said at last. "I promise."

Starbuck spurred forward to join Fernández.

A little after noon Fernández raised his hand for them to halt. They were passing through a particularly rough and broken area with great open canyons branching off in different directions. Fernández dismounted and bent down to examine the flinty surface, then began walking ahead, leading his horse as he examined the signs.

"Señor Marshal," he said, "they have split up the herd."

Starbuck swore softly and dismounted beside Fernández. The soldier was right. A portion of the horses that they were trailing had moved off to the southeast while the main body turned southwest.

"How many, do you think?" Starbuck said.

"I would say fifteen horses, perhaps more."

A few yards away the new trail ran over some softer ground. They inspected it carefully.

"Three riders?" Starbuck said.

"Four," said Fernández, pointing to one side. "One was riding apart from the others." Starbuck saw that another set of tracks was just discernible at the far edge of the patch of sand. He rode along beside it until it disappeared on the next stretch of rocky ground.

"A lookout, probably," he said. "Keeping watch while the others drove the horses."

Now Starbuck had a decision to make. Should they follow the main herd or the little group that had moved away to the southeast? He would rather follow the main body, but there was a complication.

"Sergeant," he said, "did this group break away before or after the men we fought at the river caught up with the herd?"

"Before, Señor. That is very plain."

It was not all that plain to Starbuck, but he had guessed at it, and it was an important piece of information. The survivors of the encounter at the Rio Grande would not know that neither the American nor the Mexican cavalry had followed them away from the river. They would probably think that the soldiers—American or Mexican or both—would continue to pursue them, and they would report their fears to the others when they caught up. With this warning, the bandits who had heard of the fight and the presence of the soldiers on the Mexican side of the border would undoubtedly speed up their pace, making it difficult if not impossible for any pursuer to catch up with them.

But at least four of the raiders had left the main herd and gone their own way before the rear guard had caught up; those four men would not be aware of the battle at the river or of the possible closeness of pursuit. As a result, they might continue to move in a leisurely manner, believing themselves safe now that they were across the border. They would be easier to catch, and they might have one or more of the female hostages with them.

It was a difficult decision, but Starbuck made it without hesitation.

"We'll follow this smaller bunch," he said. "They may get careless."

An hour later they came to the area where the four outlaws had camped for the night. Starbuck checked the embers of the fire and felt a tingle of anticipation sweep through him—the ashes were still warm. The bandits were not more than three or four hours ahead of them, perhaps less.

Hearing this, Kate Beaumont swung her mount around and followed the tracks out of the camp at a fast canter, headed southeastward.

"The Señora is very anxious to find these men, no?" said Fernández.

"She's very anxious to get us all killed, I think," said Starbuck. "Come on, let's catch up with her and slow her down a little."

The trail became very narrow and winding. It passed between sheer, towering cliffs cut by steep defiles and dotted with huge boulders. Every step of the way presented a hundred excellent hiding places where a man with a rifle could wait and watch the trail, and now the tingle which Starbuck felt was not anticipation but apprehension. They had to keep moving—there was no time for excessive caution—but he knew that they were pushing too hard for safety, risking their lives to close the gap more quickly between themselves and the four riders ahead of them. Yet he did not want to slow down, and he knew that Kate Beaumont did not. To hell with it, he decided. Let's gamble a little.

As they approached the top of a long rise in the trail, Fernández held up his hand again and waited for Starbuck to rein in beside him.

"Señor, I know this country fairly well," he said. "Beyond that hill is a little valley. There is a rancho there. I do not know if anyone still lives there. Indians and bandits have driven away most of those who tried to settle in this region."

"Have you ever seen the place?" Starbuck asked.

"Once, many years ago. There was a small house, a few out-buildings."

"Corral?"

"Yes," said Fernández, his eyes lighting up. "There was a large corral. The people who lived there raised and sold horses."

"Jackpot!" said Starbuck under his breath.

He and Fernández left their horses by the trail and crept slow-ly along the rimrock until they could look down into the valley. As Fernández had said, it was small, hardly more than a hollow among the cliffs. In the center of the open area was an adobe house, and next to it a large corral, recently repaired. The corral was crowded with horses. Starbuck recognized several of them.

He inspected the house carefully. The windows were heavily shuttered, and the door appeared to be thick and solid. People who built houses in that country built them for defense, not comfort. Someone was in the house; four horses were tied to the hitchrail in front, and a wisp of smoke curled upward from the chimney.

"It's going to be hard to shoot them out of there," Starbuck said to Fernández. "The place looks like a small fort. We're going to have to catch them in the open and pick off at least a couple of them before they know what's hit them. If we get into a stand-up gunfight with them it'll be bad odds—four to two."

"Four to three," said Kate Beaumont, crawling up beside them. Starbuck gazed at her for several seconds, frowned, then resumed his scrutiny of the ranchhouse.

"You sure?" he said to her.

"Just tell me what you want me to do."

"All right, would you be willing to ride up to the door of that house alone?"

"So they'll come outside?"

"Exactly. If the Sergeant or I did it, they'd shoot us down before we got within fifty yards of the place. But if a woman rides in there alone, they'll be curious, and less cautious. They may even get a little . . . greedy."

"All right."

"Kate, if anything goes wrong . . . save that last bullet."

With infinite care, Starbuck and Fernández worked their way down into the hollow. They had to circle around behind the house to find a descent that would conceal them from anyone looking out of the windows, but at last they managed it. Starbuck had considered and rejected the idea of trying to pick off the outlaws from the rimrock. It was too far for absolute accuracy, even with rifles, and if anything went wrong Kate Beaumont would be all alone down there with little chance of getting away. They had to get closer so that they could engage the bandits at point-blank range.

It took them over an hour to pick their way down the cliffs and find firing points near the ranchhouse. Fernández crept into some rocks to one side of the door, while Starbuck took up a position behind a corner of an adobe brick outbuilding on the other side. Kate Beaumont was watching their movements from the rim; when she saw that they were in position, she mounted up and rode boldly down the trail into the hollow, walking her horse slowly toward the house.

The bandits were apparently not keeping a lookout, for no one challenged her as she approached. Starbuck was holding his breath, wondering if he had made a mistake. Would they shoot her without warning?

Kate Beaumont reined up about twenty yards from the front door.

"Hello!" she called loudly. "Anybody home?"

The reaction was instantaneous; scrambling accompanied by loud curses could be heard inside the house, followed by the unmistakable sounds of weapons being readied. A shadow moved behind one of the firing ports in the shutters.

"It's a woman," said a voice. "By herself, too. Now what the hell . . . ?"

The door opened and three men walked out, pistols held at

the ready. Only three, thought Starbuck. Damn it, where's the other one?

"Well, now," said the first man, "what have we got here?"

"Must be Christmas," said the second man, licking his lips.

"Who the hell are you, lady?" said the third man.

The first two had reholstered their pistols, but the third one, more suspicious, was still holding his weapon trained on Kate Beaumont.

The fourth one, Starbuck thought. Where's the fourth one? Come on out, you. . . .

The fourth man came through the door. He was fat and shirtless and his fly was unbuttoned. He was holding a shotgun.

"What's going on?" he said, blinking in the sunlight.

Starbuck stepped out from behind the building, his Colt in his hand.

"Peace officer," he said loudly. "Drop your guns! Now!"

The first two men reached for their holsters; the fourth man gaped stupidly at Starbuck, then started to cock the shotgun.

The third man was the quickest to react; he whirled and raised his already-drawn pistol. Starbuck shot him in the chest. The gunman went over backwards into a watering trough, the six-gun flying away into the dirt.

The first man had his pistol almost clear of the leather when Fernández fired. Blood and flesh flew from the man's temple; he flopped to the ground and lay still.

The second man had bungled his draw. His thumb slipped off the hammer, and the gun fired as it was coming out of the holster, sending up a spray of sand a few inches in front of his feet. Starbuck's Colt kicked in his hand again, but the man had started to twist his body away and the bullet only hit him in the arm. The man tried to raise his pistol with his other hand, but Kate Beaumont shot him through the body with her Winchester and he dropped.

The fourth man—the one who had been the last to come out of the house—panicked and sent a charge of buckshot twenty feet over Starbuck's head. Before he could discharge the second barrel, Fernández fired again. The slug ripped the muscles of the fat man's chest, spraying blood over his arms and body. He howled in pain and stumbled back through the door; Starbuck sent a bullet through his buttocks as he disappeared into the dark interior of the house.

The door started to swing shut, and Starbuck cursed himself for not putting the man down before he got inside. Once he had barred the door, it would take a small army to blast him out. But Fernández came out of the rocks, raced across the intervening ground, and threw himself against the heavy door just as it slammed shut. It popped open again, and the momentum of Fernández' charge carried him right through the doorway into the house.

Starbuck started running for the door.

"Kate," he yelled, "get out of the line of fire!"

She wheeled the horse to one side and leaped to the ground. Starbuck was still ten paces from the open door of the house when a shotgun boomed inside. Certain that Fernández was dead, Starbuck braced himself to dive through the door before the bandit could reload, but it proved unnecessary. Fernández came out of the house holding the shotgun in one hand, a broad grin on his swarthy features.

"You all right?" Starbuck said, pulling up.

"Certainly, Señor."

"The man inside?"

"He never had many brains, I think," said Fernández. "Now he has none at all."

"You took a chance, amigo," Starbuck said.

Fernández shrugged.

"It makes life more interesting," he said indifferently.

"Grant," Kate Beaumont called, "this one's still alive." She was standing over the man Fernández had shot in the head.

They went over and stared down at him. The bullet had cut the flesh along the side of his head and taken away part of his ear, but had not penetrated the skull. He was staring up at them, still dazed from the impact of the slug.

It occurred to Starbuck that at last he was actually close enough to reach out and touch a living member of the gang which had destroyed his town and his family. The thought made him slightly sick.

"You got a name?" he said roughly.

"Go to hell," the man snarled.

Starbuck holstered his Colt, then reached down and grabbed the man by the front of his shirt. He lifted him bodily off the ground, then slammed him backwards into the wall of the house and held him there.

"Now let's try it again, you pig," Starbuck said, his face inches from the other man's. "What's your name? Or didn't your mother know?"

"Holloway," the man growled. "Deke Holloway. What's all this about, anyway?"

"Where have the rest of your gang gone?"

"I dunno what you're talkin' about," Holloway said.

Starbuck let go of him, and he crumpled into a heap against the wall, putting his hand to his head.

"You dirty greaser," Holloway said to Fernández, "you've shot my ear off."

"Watch him, Kate," said Starbuck. "If he moves, kill him. If he uses the word 'greaser' again, kill him anyway."

"It will be a pleasure," she said, covering the sitting man with the Winchester.

Starbuck and Fernández searched the dead men, then the interior of the house. There was only one large room. Half-a-dozen bunks lined the walls and a battered stove stood in one corner. In another corner lay the body of the man Fernández had killed; most of his head was missing. Starbuck threw a blanket over him and looked around. There was no sign of a hostage. If any of the kidnapped women were still alive, they must be with the main body of the outlaws.

Four sets of saddlebags had been tossed carelessly around the room; Starbuck picked them up one by one and dumped their contents onto a bunk. A gold watch fell out of one of the saddlebags onto the mattress. Starbuck picked it up. The front of the watch's cover bore the engraved initials "G.S." He stared at it, stunned.

"What is it, Señor Marshal?" Fernández asked. "Do you know this watch?"

"It's mine," Starbuck said. "The last time I saw it, it was sitting on my dresser at home, the morning that. . . ."

He opened the watch; on the inside of the cover was a faded photograph. The face of his dead wife stared out at him.

Starbuck picked up the saddlebag from which the watch had fallen. Burned into the leather were the letters "D-E-K-E."

He walked out of the door and stood in front of the wounded man.

"You said your name was 'Deke'?"

"Yeah."

Starbuck held out the saddlebags.

"Yours?"

"Yeah. So what?"

Starbuck dropped the saddlebags and drew his Colt. With his other hand he held the watch by its chain a few inches in front of the man's eyes.

"Where did you get this watch?"

"I dunno. Won it in a poker game."

"When?"

"How the hell do I know? Two, three months ago."

"What is it, Grant?" Kate Beaumont said.

Fernández answered for him.

"It is the Marshal's watch, Señora. His wife's picture is in it."

Kate Beaumont caught her breath and looked at Starbuck. The pain on his face was indescribable.

"Mister," said Starbuck, "I want you to tell me where you got this watch."

"I forget."

Starbuck pressed the muzzle of the Colt firmly against Holloway's forehead.

"Try to remember," he said.

Beads of sweat appeared on the man's brow.

"All right, all right," he snarled. "We hit a town the other side of the border a couple of days ago. One of the boys picked it up there. I traded him a couple of pistols for it while we were riding south."

"Who did you get it from?"

"Man named Whitey Sykes. What's it to you?"

"He one of these?" Starbuck said, gesturing at the bodies lying nearby.

"Hell no," said Holloway.

"Is he riding south with the others?"

"Yeah, I guess so."

"Describe him."

"Why? Who the hell are you, anyway, mister?"

Starbuck cocked the Colt.

"Describe him."

"Okay, okay, take it easy," Holloway said. "Big man, got white hair and real pale eyes. Left-handed. Never liked the son of a bitch anyway," he grumbled.

"Where are they headed?"

"Who?"

"You know who. The rest of your gang, the ones driving the other horses south. Where are they going?"

The muscles of the man's jaw tightened.

"Go to hell."

Starbuck pressed the muzzle of the Colt harder against the man's forehead, pushing his head back against the wall.

"Where are they going, Holloway?"

"Go to hell. Shoot me if you want, but I ain't tellin' you nothin' more. Nothin'!"

Starbuck waited for several seconds more, the muzzle of the Colt still hard against Holloway's head. Then, reluctantly, he pulled the gun away and eased the hammer down.

"I ought to kill you," he said, "but I won't. I'll let the law take care of you."

Holloway laughed.

"I knew you were bluffin'," he said.

Fernández cleared his throat.

"Señor Marshal," he said, "I believe that if you will allow me a few minutes alone with this man, I may be able to reason with him. Perhaps I can persuade him to provide the information that you desire."

"All right," said Starbuck, reluctantly holstering the Colt. "Go ahead. We need to know where the others are headed, and we're short on time. They've gotten too far ahead of us. If we have to keep following them by reading sign we'll never catch up to them now."

"Then if you and the Señora would care to go inside while I speak with him. . . ." Fernández suggested.

Starbuck hesitated, but Kate Beaumont stepped forward.

"Come on, Grant," she said, "let Sergeant Fernández talk with him. Let's go see what else we can find in there."

She took his arm and led him inside, giving hardly a glance at the body under the blood-soaked blanket in the corner. They finished sorting through the litter from the saddlebags, discovering more jewelry and some other things that appeared to be from the Comanche Wells raid. At the bottom of one saddlebag Starbuck found an old wanted poster; its edges were torn, and it was creased and dirty.

"This looks like the man you shot out there," he said, examining the picture. "Do you suppose the idiot carried his own wanted notice around with him? That's what I call vanity."

He went to the door to see if the picture matched the face of the dead man. As he came out of the house he stared around in surprise. Fernández was gone. So was the wounded man.

"Now where the devil. . . . ?" said Starbuck aloud.

"What's the matter?" Kate Beaumont called. She came hurrying out, the Winchester ready.

"Fernández is missing, and so is our prisoner."

"They can't have gone far," she said. "Why do you suppose. . . ."

A single, piercing scream of agony came echoing out of the

74

rocks behind the house. It rose and fell and rose again, then stopped abruptly. The sound sent a chill down Starbuck's spine. He knew immediately what had happened.

Sergeant Fernández came walking out of the rocks alone, wiping his hands on a dirty neckerchief. He tossed the rag away as he approached them.

"Marshal," he said, "I am happy to inform you that Señor Holloway decided to tell me where his friends are taking the rest of the horses. It is a place called Pueblo Rojo, a small town about thirty miles from here, beyond the next range of mountains. I am acquainted with this pueblo. It is well known as a meeting place for bandidos, especially those who have livestock or other valuables which they wish to sell."

"Where's Holloway?" Starbuck said in a thick voice. It's a stupid question, he thought; I already know the answer.

"Regrettably," said Fernández, "Señor Holloway has met with an accident. I am afraid that he is dead."

Starbuck stared at Fernández. What he had merely threatened to do, Fernández had done. He should have foreseen it, and, as a sworn officer of the law, he should have prevented it. Yet he felt nothing. Another gang member was dead. Good riddance.

Then a thought struck him, and he glanced quickly at Kate Beaumont. What would she think of him for allowing this to happen? She must be horrified.

But Kate was looking calmly at Fernández, her face twisted into a little smile.

"Lieutenant Guerrero was right, Sergeant," she murmured. "You *are* a man of many talents."

She touched Starbuck's arm.

"Come on, Grant," she said. "There's some coffee on the stove inside. Let's all go have a cup."

CHAPTER EIGHT

Presently they began preparations for resuming the chase. As it was already late afternoon they might have chosen to remain where they were for the night, but Starbuck was firm.

"My guess is that our four friends were bringing those animals here to sell to someone," he said. "Whoever the buyers are, they'll probably be along soon, and I don't want to be here when they arrive. They might not be too friendly when they find out that we've killed their associates. We'll camp somewhere along the trail."

When Kate Beaumont was momentarily out of earshot, Fernández approached Starbuck and spoke to him in a low voice.

"Señor," he said, "you are not angry with me about the dead gringo?"

Starbuck gave him a thin smile.

"No, Sergeant," he said, "I'm not angry with you. You just did what I wanted to do myself."

He glanced down at Fernández' Army uniform.

"However," he said, "if we're going to Pueblo Rojo we'd better find you some other clothes."

"Yes," said Fernández, laughing. "I do not think I would live long in a place like Pueblo Rojo dressed like this."

Inside the house they found him some suitable items of clothing among the belongings of the dead men. He changed into them quickly.

"We can't keep calling you 'Sergeant,' either," Starbuck said.

"My given name is Diego," suggested Fernández.

"Good. Mine's Grant."

Kate Beaumont came in.

"What are we going to do about the horses?" she asked.

"We'll have to let them go," Starbuck said. "We can't drive them with us and we can't leave them to starve in the corral. Running loose, they'll manage until someone comes."

"I'll open the gate," she said, and went out.

Starbuck went to the spring to fill the canteens. Presently he heard the creak of the corral gate, and the restless movement of the horses as they realized that they were free. Suddenly Kate Beaumont cried out. Starbuck whirled and was astonished to see her standing in the middle of the corral with her arms about the neck of a young chestnut mare. The other horses were pushing past her, all trying to get out of the gate at once, but the mare remained still as Kate stood there hugging her.

"What's going on?" Starbuck said, dodging the other horses as he walked up to the corral.

"Oh, Grant," Kate said. "She's mine . . . my own saddle horse. They took her from the ranch. I never thought I'd see her again."

Starbuck saw that there were tears in her eyes. The woman who had cold-bloodedly killed two men and was seeking the death of many more was crying with joy at being reunited with an animal that she had loved. She has reason enough to be happy, thought Starbuck. It's the first decent thing that's happened to her since this whole horrible nightmare began.

"I'll get your saddle and gear from the other horse," he said.

They took what food and ammunition they could find. Fernández appropriated the fat man's shotgun, and they each now had a spare six-gun or two tucked away in their saddlebags. Starbuck had three.

No one suggested burying the dead outlaws.

Within the hour they were climbing the trail away from the little valley. Only when they had put many miles behind them did Starbuck begin to breathe easier.

They rode south until the last light of the sunset started to fade from the highest peaks, then left the trail and climbed through the rocks until they found an acceptable place to spend the night. Several hundred yards up the slope they came upon a long overhanging ledge which formed a natural shelter flanked on both sides by huge boulders. They would be well hidden from anyone riding along the trail below, and well protected from any attack if one should come.

They unrolled their blankets and sat beneath the ledge, making a spartan meal from dried beef and stale bread. There was no water, but they drank a little from the canteens and gave some to the horses. They dared not make a fire.

After they had eaten they talked a little, keeping their voices low so that the sound would not carry too far among the rocks.

"Captain Lattimer told me that you used to be a Texas Ranger," Kate Beaumont said to Starbuck.

"Yes. That was a long time ago."

"Why did you leave the Rangers to become a town marshal?" she asked.

Starbuck hesitated.

"I wanted a home and a family," he said. "Being a Ranger was no life for a married man."

Kate Beaumont bit her lip. She had not meant to remind him of his dead wife and children. She turned to Fernández.

"Are you married, Diego?" she said.

"No, Señora."

"It is good of you to help us like this," she said.

"It is my pleasure, Señora. It was Teniente Guerrero's wish, and I am happy to serve him by serving you."

He paused, then continued.

"There is another reason that I am glad of the opportunity to go with you," he said. "You asked me if I was married. I *was* married, once. My wife was killed three years ago when bandidos attacked the hacienda of my patrón . . . Teniente Guerrero's father. He was killed too. So you see, like you, Teniente Guerrero and I know what it is like to lose a loved one. And he and I know what it is like to hate those who take our loved ones from us. We understand your sorrow."

He got up.

"If you will forgive me, I think that I will rest now. Tomorrow we will reach Pueblo Rojo, and there will be much to do there."

He moved away to the far end of the ledge, rolled himself in his blanket, and was soon asleep.

"A strange man," Kate Beaumont said.

"Not so strange, when you think about it," Starbuck said. "This is a hard land, Kate. Harder even than where you and I come from, across the border. He's a product of the world he lives in."

"Some world. Did you hear that man scream today?"

"We needed information," Starbuck said, "and Diego got it. He's a realist, that's all."

"What about you, Grant?" she said. "Are you a realist too?"

He thought for a moment.

"You know," he said heavily, "I never thought of myself as a hard or violent or evil man. But in the past three days I've killed seven men, and I don't feel a thing. Not pity, not remorse, not anything. All I want is to find the men we're chasing and kill them too."

"I know," she said. "I feel the same way. I should be feeling horror or regret for what we've done, but I don't. What's happening to us, Grant? What have we become?"

"Avengers, Kate. For us that's the only reality now."

"And afterwards? What becomes of us afterwards?"

"That's easy. For us there isn't going to be an afterwards. We're going to die in Mexico."

"You think we have no chance at all?"

"Of doing what we came to do and still getting out alive? No. None."

"Do you want to turn back?"

"No. Do you?"

"No."

"Good night, Kate."

"Good night, Grant."

Presently they slept.

CHAPTER NINE

They reached Pueblo Rojo at midday. The town lay in a wide, barren valley surrounded by brooding mountains. Starbuck thought that he had never before seen such a large community in such a desolate place. The pueblo had an appearance of timelessness, as if it had been there for centuries . . . as in fact it had. Indians, conquistadors, missionaries, settlers, bandits—each had come in turn to Pueblo Rojo, each in turn impressing their distinctive mark upon it. The varied architecture of the town reflected the diversity of those who had brought their dreams to the pueblo, lived there briefly, and then passed on, often leaving their bones behind in the iron-hard soil.

Starbuck's nerves were on edge as they rode slowly through the dusty streets toward the center of the town. Knowing why he had come, he instinctively feared that others would sense it too, and react accordingly. But no one paid them the slightest heed; the people that they passed went about their affairs without even glancing at them as they rode by. It dawned on Starbuck then that the residents of Pueblo Rojo were used to the arrival of strangers, and knew better than to take too great an interest in their business there. Fernández had said that the town was a refuge for bandits and a marketplace for their wares, and in such a place it would not be healthy to wonder too much about a stranger or the stranger's reasons for being there. The towns-people were deliberately taking no notice of them.

It was an eerie feeling, being ignored like that as they rode along—almost as if they were invisible. Starbuck relaxed a little, but only a little. He knew that at any moment they might encounter someone, perhaps one of the bandits that he had fought at the river, or even someone from further back in his past, who might recognize him. If that happened, he and his companions would be fortunate to escape from Pueblo Rojo alive.

He saw also that this was not the type of settlement where one might find a livery stable, a hotel, or a restaurant. The men who came to Pueblo Rojo did not want such things, and the people who lived there did not need them. In a way, Starbuck thought, the place was like some of the cattle towns where he had served as a lawman in his earlier days, a place where men came only to drink and fight and whore; to be safe from pursuit for a little while, to dispose of their ill-gotten gains, and then ride on again. The three of them might be invisible now, but soon they would begin to stick out like sore thumbs as it became plain that they had come for none of these things.

"Diego," he said to Fernández, "we've got to find a place where we can put up, get some food, and be reasonably safe while we look the town over and get our ears to the ground. It may take us awhile to find the men we're searching for."

"I have been thinking much the same thing, Señor. But that will not be so easy here, I think. I believe that there is only one place in this pueblo where we might safely stay."

"Where's that?"

Fernández pointed. Ahead of them rose the twin bell towers of a Spanish mission church.

"There," he said. "Perhaps our Holy Mother the Church will give us sanctuary."

The mission was a large one, surrounded by a high wall of ancient adobe which hid much of the mission from view as they approached. There was, however, a huge wrought-iron gate through which they could see the buildings and portions of the spacious grounds within.

Fernández led them up to the gate, leaned over from his saddle, and pulled vigorously on a bell-rope which hung near the gatepost. On the other side of the wall a bell pealed, and within moments an elderly priest dressed in a flowing brown robe appeared behind the gate.

"What is it that you wish, my children?" he said.

"We seek sanctuary for the night, Padre," said Fernández.

The priest looked keenly at them, observing their travel-stained clothes, worn horses, and tense features. His gaze rested on Kate Beaumont momentarily, as he noted her haggard face and haunted eyes.

"Sanctuary?" he said. "You are in danger, then?"

"Yes, Padre," said Fernández.

"And you cannot find a place of rest in the town?"

"We are not of this town, Padre, and we cannot be seen by too many of the people in it. The lady especially is in great danger. We need your help, and we are not destitute. We would be honored if you would allow us to contribute handsomely to your poor box before we leave."

"If you come in peace," said the priest, "then you are welcome."

"We come in peace to you, Padre," said Fernández. Starbuck wondered if the sergeant would have to do penance later for having told this half-truth to a man of the Church.

The priest twisted a key in a heavy lock and swung back the gate. They rode through, and he shut and locked it again.

"I am Father Paul," he said. "If you will follow me, I will arrange for the care of your horses and we will then gladly share with you what little we have."

He led them to a stable near the mission buildings; as they dismounted, three peons appeared and took the horses from them. The men removed the saddles, bedrolls, and saddlebags from the horses' backs, and then led the horses away. Three more campesinos appeared, collected the gear, and then followed behind with it as the priest showed the travelers to their quarters. If the good father noticed the exceptionally large number of weapons that his three guests were carrying with them into the mission he made no mention of it.

The interior of the building was cool and dark. Father Paul showed them to their rooms—small, whitewashed cubicles furnished only with a bed, a washstand, a chair or two, and a crucifix upon the wall. A woman brought water and filled the pitchers which stood upon each washstand.

"Refresh yourselves, my children," said Father Paul. "You are tired from your journey. I will go and tell the cook to prepare something for you to eat, and will return shortly to show you to our table."

Starbuck placed his gear carefully in one corner, then closed the door and sat down upon the bed. It was quiet in the little room; sunlight filtered through the narrow window, and beyond it he caught a glimpse of flowering bushes. The scent of the flowers came faintly to him through the window, and he heard bees humming as they foraged among the blossoms.

Truly, he thought, this is a sanctuary.

Then he remembered how temporary the sanctuary must be. He took his Colt out of its holster and carefully began to clean the dust of the trail from its ivory handle and blue-steel surfaces.

Dinner was served upon a bare wooden table in a small dining room adjacent to the sleeping rooms. It was a simple affair, and after the grace was said the meal was eaten largely in silence. Two younger priests of the mission, Father Manuel and Father Carlos, ate with them.

It was only after they had finished eating and the plates had been taken away that Starbuck signalled Fernández to begin questioning the priest about the affairs of the town.

"Padre," said Fernández, "if we wished to buy horses—many horses—in Pueblo Rojo, where would we go?"

The priest frowned.

"Well, my son," he said, "if you were not too particular about where the horses came from, you would undoubtedly go to the corrals at the southern end of the town. Many animals are brought there to be sold by men who have somehow acquired more horses than they need."

"And whom should we ask for there, Padre?" said Fernández.

"The horses belong to many different men, but the man to speak to would be Rafael Ortega. He acts as the agent of those who bring the horses there to sell."

"Thank you Father," said Starbuck, rising from the table. "If you'll excuse us now, we'll go and see these corrals that you speak of."

"It is the hour of siesta, my son. It will be difficult to do business at this time of the day."

"Regrettably, Father, we must go anyway. Our time here may be short. Very short."

They rode through the town to the corrals. The pens were full; perhaps a hundred horses or more were gathered there in a dozen different enclosures.

They rode slowly among the corrals, examining the various herds.

"Do you recognize any of them?" Fernández asked at length.

"No," said Starbuck. "Any of 'em yours, Kate?"

"No. We only had three horses, and I'm riding one of them. I don't see the other two."

"Wait," said Starbuck, reining up. "That dappled gray there, and the bay next to him. I think I've seen them both before. Yes, the gray is old Pete Warner's horse. It was stolen during the raid."

He moved closer to the fence and peered through the dust at the animals in the corral.

"I'm not sure about the bay," he said. "If he'd just turn this way. . . . Yes, I'm sure now. See the "M-Bar-S" brand and the white mark across his nose? Mike Spencer got drunk one night and ran him into a wire fence in the dark. Cut his face. Cut Mike up some too."

He walked the buckskin along the corral fence, inspecting the other horses. Several of the brands were known to him.

"Couldn't swear to all them," he said, "but most of them are from Comanche Wells or ranches around there. It's the bunch we were trailing, all right. We've found them!"

"Are you sure, Grant?" Kate Beaumont said, her voice strained. "Are these really the ones we've been following so long?"

"Yes. No doubt of it. End of the trail, Kate. Or at least the beginning of the end."

"Can I be of assistance to you, my friends?" said an oily voice behind them.

A rotund man in a large sombrero was standing about twenty feet away, watching them with small, greedy eyes. He swept the sombrero off and bowed.

"Buenos días, Señora, Señores," he said. "I am Rafael Ortega, at your service."

"Good day, Señor," said Starbuck, leaning forward in the saddle, his arms resting on the saddle horn. "You can indeed help us. We're looking for horses to buy, and you have some fine animals here."

"Thank you, Señor. Are there any which interest you especially?"

"Several. For example, that gray and the big bay over there seem sound enough. The roan there, and that sorrel. . . . In fact, I'd be interested in purchasing all of the horses in this corral."

"All?" said Ortega. There was a gleam of avarice in his eye, for there were over thirty horses in the enclosure which Starbuck had indicated.

"Yes. Can you tell me where I can find their owner?"

"Ah, but you do not need to find the owner, Señor. I, Rafael Ortega, am commissioned to sell any of these horses to you."

"I understand, Señor," said Starbuck, "and of course it's with you that I'll conclude the purchase and to you that I'll pay the agreed price. But there is one difficulty—I need to inquire about the, ah, pedigree of the animals. It would be most unfortunate for me if the wrong people were to recognize any of these horses while they're in my possession. It would be much better for my health if I were to speak with the owner to make certain that I won't be taking the animals anywhere near their original homes. You understand, I hope?"

Ortega did not appear especially pleased; clearly he did not want any prospective buyers to get away, even temporarily. No doubt, thought Starbuck, he's afraid that I'll make my own deal with the men who brought them here and cut him out of his commission.

And there was a glint of suspicion in Ortega's eye; perhaps he was not persuaded that Starbuck's reason was the true one. It would not be usual for a buyer to inquire about the history of an animal which had been brought to Pueblo Rojo to be sold, and it might not be unprecedented for an angry former owner to come searching for his stolen stock here. Starbuck cursed himself for not producing a more convincing story, but it was too late now. Yet there was a way to encourage Ortega's cooperation, whatever his suspicions might be.

"This is so important to me that I'm prepared to reward you for your assistance in the matter," Starbuck said. He leaned over and placed several gold coins in Ortega's sweaty palm. Ortega beamed.

"The owner, Señor?" Starbuck prompted him.

"You will come back here to conclude the sale?" Ortega said, biting one of the coins.

"Of course. You have my word."

"Then, I believe that at this hour you will find the owners of these animals at the cantina in the plaza."

"And the man to ask for is. . . . ?"

"Ask for Señor Smith," said Ortega with a smirk. "Of course, we have many Americanos named Smith here in Pueblo Rojo, but no doubt you will find the right one."

As they rode off toward the plaza, Ortega stood watching them intently, his hands upon his hips.

"He's suspicious," said Kate Beaumont.

"Yes," said Starbuck. "Diego, I think that it might be well if you could slip back there and make certain that Señor Ortega doesn't send word ahead of us to the cantina. In fact," he added, looking Fernández in the eye, "it would be better if he were to be unable to speak to anyone for the next several hours."

"I will arrange it, Señor," said Fernández.

"Thank you, Diego. The Señora and I will wait for you in the plaza. Then we'll enter the cantina together."

"Good. I will not be long."

Starbuck and Kate Beaumont rode into the plaza and tethered their horses near the little fountain which graced the center of the square. No water flowed in the fountain; perhaps it had once, but in present-day Pueblo Rojo water was too precious to waste in fountains.

"There's the cantina," Kate said.

The cantina stood at the corner of one of the streets leading into the square. It was a large building, made of adobe brick as were most of the buildings of the town. The front door opened onto the plaza; another door was visible along the street side. The back would probably have a door too, Starbuck reflected. The hitch rail in front of the cantina was crowded with horses—apparently many of the local citizens were spending their siesta hour drinking.

"Kate," he said, "several of those horses at the hitch rail are from up around Comanche Wells. Some of the gang are in there, all right."

Presently Fernández rode up and dismounted beside the fountain. Starbuck noted that Fernández had a shotgun concealed under his duster.

"Any trouble?" Starbuck said.

"No, none. Señor Ortega was easy to deal with. The men in the cantina will be more difficult."

Starbuck slid the rawhide thong off the hammer of the Colt. Then, standing between the horses so that he could not be observed by any passerby, he reached into his saddlebag and slipped a second six-gun into his waistband. His pulse was racing. "Let's go get ourselves a drink," he said.

They walked toward the front door of the cantina. As they passed the hitchrail, Starbuck touched Kate Beaumont's arm.

"Kate," he said in a low voice, "take a look at the prints left by the right front hoof of that pinto. That animal's got a twisted frog on the right front shoe."

"Like the prints at the ranch!" she said. There was a note of triumph in her voice.

"Yes. They're in there, Kate. We've found them—some of them, anyway."

"Come on," she said, hurrying toward the door.

The cantina was crowded and noisy. Starbuck checked the room quickly, noting the location of the side and back doors. There were a few empty tables in the cantina, but the majority were occupied. Almost all of the people present were men, but there were a few women, most of whom were clearly employees of the cantina.

Starbuck noted uneasily that many of the men were Americans. Even though Pueblo Rojo was a frequent destination for fugitive gringos, it was surprising to see such a large gathering of them in one place. Presumably they had come there together, and Starbuck's skin crawled as he realized that these men were almost certainly some of those who had raided and burned Comanche Wells and Kate Beaumont's ranch.

As they entered the cantina the room fell silent as everyone in the place ceased their conversations and turned to look at them. The stares were not friendly.

"Diego, take Mrs. Beaumont to a table, will you?" Starbuck said.

He walked up to the bar as Fernández guided Kate to a table at the back of the room.

Gradually the conversations began again, but Starbuck knew that many in the cantina were still watching the three of them furtively.

"Good day, my friend," Starbuck said to the bartender. "Señor Ortega at the corrals said that I might find the owner of some horses here. His name is Mr. Smith. Can you point him out to me?"

The bartender scowled at him without replying. The other

men standing along the bar suddenly began drifting away from it, leaving its entire length clear.

"I'm Smith," said someone.

Starbuck turned. A man was leaning against the far end of the bar, facing him. Although his manner was relaxed, Starbuck could see that he was alert, his thumb hooked in his gunbelt near his holster.

Starbuck surveyed the man with care. He was tall, and his eyes were pale, almost pink, giving them a curious dead-fish appearance. Beneath his hat an untidy length of snow-white hair fell to his shoulders. And his holster was hung on the left side of his gunbelt. Starbuck heard in the back of his mind, as from a great distance, the words of the doomed man sitting on the ground in front of the little ranchhouse the day before as Starbuck had questioned him about the watch.

"Big man," he had said. "Got white hair and real pale eyes. Left-handed. . . ."

It could be, it *had* to be the same man. The man who had taken Starbuck's watch from the dresser of his bedroom in Comanche Wells. The man who had killed his family.

Starbuck went a little mad then. All logic, all reason, all caution suddenly left him. He forgot about Kate, he forgot about Fernández, he forgot about himself and where he was, he forgot that he stood in the middle of a room filled with men who could and would kill him without the slightest hesitation. All that he could see or think about was the man with the pale eyes standing before him.

He walked down the bar until he was within a yard of the white-haired man. As he moved a strange numbness descended upon him; he was conscious now of nothing but the weight of the blue-steel Colt at his hip and the baleful glare of the pink fish-eyes staring coldly back at him.

"Hello, Whitey," he said.

"How do you know my name?" said the other. "We cross trails somewhere before?"

"Oh, we've never met," Starbuck said. "But we've crossed

trails all right. Matter of fact, you were a house guest of mine recently."

"What the hell are you talking about? Where was this, anyway?"

Starbuck smiled thinly, watching the pale eyes.

"Place called Comanche Wells," he said.

Every man in the room went rigid. Gasps, a few curses, and the sudden scrape of chairs told Starbuck that his guess had been right—these were the men. And now they knew that he had come for them. They would never let him leave the cantina alive.

"Freeze!"

Fernández' voice cracked through the cantina like a whip. He was standing at the rear of the room with his back to the wall, the shotgun in his hands as he swept the room with its twin muzzles.

"The first man who reaches for a gun, dies. Stay still, amigos, and live a little longer."

The pale man's pink eyes flicked over at Fernández, then back to Starbuck.

"Just who the hell *are* you, Mister?" he said.

Slowly and deliberately, his eyes never leaving the other man's, Starbuck reached into his pocket with his left hand and pulled out the watch. He dangled it by his chain in front of the pale man's face.

"Recognize it?"

"Why should I?"

"You took it from my home in Comanche Wells the day you burned the town."

"The hell you say."

Starbuck opened the watch's cover.

"The woman in the picture," he said. "Recognize her?"

"No. Should I?"

"My wife. She was in the house when you burned it down. She and my two sons. You do remember them, don't you Whitey?"

"What the hell do you want, mister?"

"I'm going to kill you, Sykes. Just the way you killed my family."

"You must be loco," Sykes snorted. "There are a dozen men in this room who'd like to nail you to the wall right now and peel the hide right off you. You're as good as dead, Mister."

"Maybe. But my compadre back there has a shotgun on your friends, and several other weapons handy. If your little playmates try to interfere, a lot of them are going to die. And I'll get you, Whitey. Don't forget that. No matter what else happens, I'll get you before I go down."

"Damn it, who are you?"

"The man who's going to kill you."

"He's Grant Starbuck, the Marshal of Comanche Wells, Texas," said Kate Beaumont from the back of the room. "And I've got a shotgun too." The click of the hammers being cocked was loud in the stillness.

"Kate, get out of here," Starbuck said sharply. "You too, Diego. Go. Ride."

"No," said Kate Beaumont.

"No, Señor," said Fernández.

Starbuck knew that it was useless to argue, and that it was too late to save his friends in any case. He had signed their death warrants as well as his own. Well, it couldn't be helped now.

"Any time, Whitey," he said.

Sykes hesitated. Starbuck was standing only three feet away from him, and Sykes knew that at that distance even if he got a bullet into Starbuck first, the lawman would probably still be able to get off one shot, maybe two, at point-blank range. More than once both participants had died in gunfights at that distance, because neither antagonist could miss.

"What's the matter, Whitey?" Starbuck said. "Waiting for your friends to save you? Draw or crawl—it's all the same to me."

The pale man shouted an obscenity as his hand darted toward his holster. Faster than thought Starbuck brought the Colt up, cocked and ready. He had the gun's muzzle jammed into Sykes' belly long before the other man could bring his own weapon into firing position. Sykes froze, his gun only half-cocked, its barrel still pointed at the floor. For a moment time stood still as he hung there, sweating profusely and trying to decide whether to drop the gun or to shoot it out.

"Time to die, Whitey," Starbuck said softly.

The pale man made his choice. He jerked the hammer of his six-gun the rest of the way back and tried to bring the weapon up. Starbuck fired. The outlaw screamed and staggered back, clutching at himself. Starbuck shot him again; the bullet smashed through the man's blood-covered hands and into his entrails, tearing them apart. Sykes went down on his back, the scream now a shrill shriek. Starbuck stepped forward and put the third bullet through the dying man's open mouth. The shriek stopped abruptly.

The room erupted in chaos. Half of the men present scrambled for the doors; two dived through the windows in a crash of splintered glass. The rest went for their guns.

Fernández cut down three of them before their weapons cleared their holsters; Kate Beaumont's shotgun knocked another two into a heap beside them. Starbuck shot the bartender as he was reaching under the bar for something—Starbuck was not sure what and didn't care. A bullet grazed his ear and he whirled and drove a slug into the shooter's chest, then put another shot into the pelvis of a man who was lining up his pistol on Fernández.

His Colt was empty now, and he shifted it smoothly to his left hand as with his right he drew the other six-gun from his waistband.

"Everybody hold it right there!" he roared.

Less than five seconds had passed since Whitey went for his gun. Several men stood paralyzed with indecision, some crouched with their weapons half-drawn. There was shock and fear in all of their faces. Hard men though they were, they were stunned by the swiftness of what they had just seen. Frozen in uncertainty they stared at Starbuck, at the cocked six-gun in his hand, and at the dead and wounded men scattered about the blood-smeared barroom floor.

"Grant!" screamed Kate Beaumont. Starbuck whirled.

A short, wiry man in a fringed leather shirt had stepped around Kate and twisted the shotgun out of her hands. Now he was standing behind her with his left arm tight around her neck and a pistol pressed hard against her right ear.

"Don't move, either of you," the man shouted to Starbuck and Fernández. "If you twitch, she dies."

The gunman started to move back toward the rear door of the cantina, pulling Kate with him. Kate was yanking at the arm around her throat, but the man was too strong for her to pull loose from him.

"Stop that, you slut!" the man snarled. "Stop it or I'll blow your head off!"

Starbuck knew that at all costs he must not let the man take Kate out that door. He remembered vividly what had happened to the women on the trail; he could not let it happen to her. She would be better off dead. He raised the six-gun and pointed it at the gunman's head.

"I'll kill her!" the man cried, seeing the movement.

"You'll kill her anyway," Starbuck said. "I've seen what you and your friends do to women, and I'd rather have her die now than later after you've gotten through with her. So we might as well get it over with."

"Shoot, Grant, shoot!" Kate Beaumont cried.

Starbuck started to squeeze the trigger, and found that he could not. He couldn't help it. He did not want Kate Beaumont to die.

Seeing his hesitation, Kate Beaumont slammed her elbow back into the gunman's ribs, then jerked her head down and sank her teeth deep into the man's left forearm. The man howled in pain, then lowered his six-gun, jammed it into the small of her back, and pulled the trigger. The bullet tore through her body and exploded out the front of her shirt. Kate Beaumont lurched forward, her face twisted in agony, blood soaking her clothing.

Starbuck let out a shout of rage and shot the gunman through the face, blowing away his lower jaw. The man slumped to the floor, moaning and gagging. Consumed by his fury, Starbuck stepped forward and put four bullets into the man's lower belly, then shot him through the heart.

Jamming new cartridges rapidly into the Colt, Starbuck looked around for any remaining opposition, but all of the rest of the cantina's occupants had long since bolted out of the building.

Fernández was kneeling over Kate Beaumont where she lay on the floor. Starbuck dropped to his knees beside her. She was conscious, her eyes open. Her lips formed words, but no sound came. Blood was flowing profusely from her wounds.

Starbuck grabbed a dishtowel from behind the bar and tore it into several lengths, then tied them together and wrapped them tightly around her body. Within seconds, the rags were sodden with blood. Kate Beaumont was bleeding to death before his eyes.

"We've got to get her out of here," he said to Fernández. "If we can get her back to the mission quick enough, she may have a chance. I'll carry her, you cover us."

He lifted her up in his arms and started toward the front door. Fernández followed, reloading the shotgun. As they came out of the door, several gunshots echoed across the plaza. Bullets slapped into the adobe walls and ripped splinters off the wooden doorframe inches from their heads. They ducked back into the cantina and flattened themselves against the wall near the doorway.

"We've got to do something," Starbuck said, looking down at Kate, who had now lost consciousness. "If we don't get her some help quickly, she's going to die."

He laid her gently on the floor, then pulled out his Colt and checked the cylinder carefully.

"I'm going out there, Diego," he said. "While I'm keeping them busy, you get her to the horses and ride like hell for the mission. Never mind about me. Just save her!"

Fernández reached out and touched his arm.

"We will save her together, amigo," he said.

Before Starbuck could stop him, Fernández was on his feet,

dashing through the front door. Gunfire erupted in the plaza again as he came bursting out of the cantina. Starbuck shouted a warning to Fernández, then swung Kate Beaumont's limp form over his shoulder and stumbled after him.

They ran for the horses, Fernández in front; the Mexican was like a mad bull, roaring curses as he fired first to one side and then the other. When the shotgun was empty he hurled it from him and drew both of his pistols, shooting at anything which moved in the plaza. In seconds they had reached the horses; bullets slapped off the stones of the fountain as Starbuck swung up onto the buckskin's back, Kate still slung over his shoulder like a sack of meal. He feared that the rough handling would aggravate her wounds, but he had no choice. The only chance now was to get her away from the plaza.

Fernández was aboard his own horse, still shooting like a madman. Starbuck spurred the buckskin hard, and the startled animal leaped into action, plunging headlong across the plaza with Starbuck desperately hanging onto Kate Beaumont and praying that she would not be hit again by the bullets which were snapping past them. Her chestnut mare, maddened with fear, broke free from the hitchrail and galloped riderless after them.

Fernández was behind them, keeping his body between the two of them and the gunmen in the plaza. As he rode, Fernández was firing back at their antagonists with still another pistol which he had pulled out of his saddlebag as he mounted up. Starbuck heard him grunt once in pain, but then he began shooting again. His horse stayed close behind Starbuck's buckskin as they raced out of the plaza and galloped madly down the narrow streets toward the mission. Starbuck glanced back, but there was no sign of pursuit. For the moment at least, they were safe.

The priest was at the gate; perhaps he had heard the gunfire and had expected something of the sort. He swung the gate open and the three horses passed through. Slamming the gate and locking it, the priest ran after them toward the mission.

A dozen peons ran to help; Starbuck handed Kate gently down to them.

"Take her inside, quickly!" said the priest.

They put her on the bed in her room. Her clothing was now soaked with blood.

"Is she alive?" Starbuck asked in an agonized voice.

"Yes," said the priest. "She is unconscious, but she is still alive."

"Can you save her?" Starbuck said.

"Only God can save her," said the priest. "I will use all my skill, Señor, but it is in His hands."

He tore away part of the bloody shirt and examined the wounds with great care.

"It is an ugly wound," he said presently, "but it does not appear that anything vital has been touched."

"Will she be all right?"

"I can promise nothing. She has lost much blood, but I believe that we may be in time. It is fortunate that you were able to get her here so quickly."

There was a sound behind them. Fernández was standing in the doorway, leaning against the doorframe.

"She will live?" Fernández said, his eyes on the bed where Kate Beaumont lay.

"I think so," said Starbuck, "thanks to you. If you hadn't done what you did, we'd never have gotten her out of that place in time. You saved her life, amigo."

"Then I am content," Fernández said. He coughed, then pitched forward and lay face down on the floor.

Starbuck knelt beside him, appalled. There were three gaping bullet holes in Fernández' back. Two of the wounds bubbled forth a bloody froth each time Fernández breathed, and blood was trickling from the corner of his mouth.

"Father!" Starbuck cried, lifting Fernández' head up and cushioning it on his arm.

The priest hurried over, examined the fallen man quickly, then lifted his eyes to meet Starbuck's.

"There is nothing that I can do for him," he said. "The bullets have pierced his lungs. He is dying."

He rose and spoke to one of the women who were rushing in with water and bandages.

"Get Father Manuel," he said. "We have a man here who needs the last rites." He went back to Kate Beaumont's bedside, rolled up his sleeves, and set to work.

Starbuck rolled Fernández over onto his back, then placed a blanket over him and gently slid a pillow beneath his head. Fernández was conscious, but seemed to be in no pain.

"Señor Starbuck, will you do me one small favor?" he whispered. His breath was becoming labored, irregular.

"Anything, Diego," Starbuck said. "Anything."

"Would you be so good as to tell Teniente Guerrero that I did my best to carry out his orders?"

"I'll tell him."

"I did well, didn't I, Señor Starbuck?"

"You did very well, my friend. No man could have done better. Teniente Guerrero will be proud of you. So am I."

"Thank you, Señor," Fernández said. He coughed again.

"Good-bye, Señor Starbuck," he gasped.

"Good-bye, Diego. Vaya con Dios."

"Vayan con Dios, Señor Starbuck," Fernández murmured. "You and the Señora."

He closed his eyes and died.

Starbuck slowly rose to his feet. He was suddenly very tired. Father Paul looked up from his place by Kate Beaumont's bed.

"Is he dead?"

"Yes, Father," Starbuck said. Wearily, he picked up his rifle. "I'd better get back outside," he said. "I don't think that they followed us, but if they did there'll be more trouble. I'm sorry to have brought all of this upon you."

"Do not worry, my son. Trouble is no stranger to us. But I do not think that the bandidos will bother us here. Even if they know where you are, they will not invade holy ground."

"I don't think that these men fear God, or even believe in Him," Starbuck said. "Anyway, I'd better go and keep watch, just in case."

But no one came after them. Either the gunmen did not know where they had gone, or, as the priest had said, they did not dare to violate the sanctity of the mission. At dusk, with all still quiet, Starbuck gave up his vigil and returned to Kate Beaumont's room. He found Father Paul sitting beside her bed, fingering his rosary. "How is she, Father?" he said.

"She is sleeping. I gave her some laudanum."

"How serious is the wound?"

"It is a miracle," said the priest. "When the bullet entered her back it struck a rib and followed the bone around, coming out cleanly through the flesh of her side. It touched no vital organ. It did not even break the rib. I have heard of such things, but I have never seen it before."

He rose and stared down at the sleeping woman.

"The chief danger to her now is the loss of blood and the shock which follows any serious wound. She is very weak."

He gave Starbuck a thin smile.

"You and Señor Fernández did well to get her here alive," he said. "She is fortunate to have had such brave friends."

"I got her into the trouble to begin with," Starbuck said. "It's my fault that she's hurt and that Fernández is dead."

He leaned his rifle in a corner and sat down in a chair beside Kate Beaumont's bed. He longed to close his eyes and sleep.

"I have sent one of our people to the plaza to watch and listen," said the priest. "The men with whom you fought have ridden away. They will not bother you again. Not here, not for the present at least. You may rest now, if you wish."

Starbuck gazed at the still figure on the bed.

"I'd like to sit with her awhile if it's all right, Father," he said.

"Of course, my son," said the priest.

For a long time Starbuck sat in the chair, unmoving, watching Kate Beaumont's sleeping form. Finally weariness overcame him, and he slept.

CHAPTER TEN

Shortly after daylight, Father Paul slipped quietly back into the room. The slight creak of the door opening woke Starbuck; he came up out of the chair wild-eyed, Colt in hand. He had been dreaming of blood and death.

"I'm sorry, Father," he said sheepishly, reholstering the Colt and sinking back into the chair.

"Have I been here all night?" he asked, blinking in the morning sunlight which poured through the window.

The priest knelt by Kate Beaumont, then rose and smiled down at Starbuck.

"I thought it best to let you sleep," he said. "I came during the night to check on both of you."

"How is she?"

"Stronger, I think. Her color is better, and her breathing and pulse are nearly normal."

"I'm deeply grateful to you, Father. Without you she would have died. Your skill saved her."

"I cannot take the credit, my son. God saved Señora Beaumont's life, not I. I was but His instrument."

Starbuck walked to the window and looked out at the flowering bush and the mission grounds beyond.

"Father," he said, "those men that we fought in the plaza, the men we followed here from the border. Do you know who they were?"

"Yes. The story of your encounter with them is all over town this morning."

"Who were they?"

"I fear that they were Pierre LeCoq's men."

"LeCoq? Who's he?"

"A Frenchman, a mercenary who served as an officer in the Emperor Maximilian's army when the French ruled Mexico. When Maximilian was defeated and executed, LeCoq fled to the mountains and gathered together an army of his own, an army of renegades like himself. He is a dangerous man, my son. A very dangerous man."

"Where's his headquarters?"

"To the south, in the Sierra Oscura—the Dark Mountains."

"How far?"

"A day's ride, no more."

"Where in the mountains, Father?"

"He has built a stronghold in a place which the Indians in their superstition have named 'Guarida Diablo.'"

"'The Devil's Lair,'" said Starbuck. "Very dramatic."

"Perhaps," said the priest. "But make no mistake—this LeCoq is a devil, a devil in human form. He has at least fifty or sixty men at his command, a legion of misfits, outlaws, and deserters, the worst bandits and cutthroats in all of Mexico. They ride where they please and do as they please, stealing and killing as the fancy takes them. No one can stand against them. No one. You have chosen a powerful enemy, my son."

"I didn't choose him, Father," said Starbuck. "He chose me."

They buried Diego Fernández in a shady corner of the mission grounds, beneath the spreading branches of an aged tree. The rites were spoken in Latin, of course, but though Starbuck did not understand the words he was moved by the dignity of the ancient ritual and felt comforted by it. He thought that Diego Fernández would have been pleased.

When it was done, Starbuck approached Father Paul.

"Father," he said, "is there a stonemason in the town?"

"Yes, a very good one."

"I'd like to have him carve a headstone for Sergeant Fernández' grave. I'll pay for it, of course. Can you arrange it for me?"

"Certainly," said the priest. "It is most thoughtful of you."

Starbuck reached into his shirt and handed the priest a letter.

"This letter tells of all that has happened since Señora Beaumont and I entered Mexico," he said. "If you could have one of your people carry it as soon as possible to Teniente Roberto Guerrero at the Presidio at Rio del Norte, I would be most grateful."

"It will be on its way within the hour."

"Thank you, Father."

"And you, my son?"

"I have to go, Father."

"To find LeCoq?"

"Yes."

"To kill him?"

"Yes. If I can."

"It is wrong to kill."

"My family was killed. My friends and neighbors were killed. Señora Beaumont's husband was killed."

"But you have already destroyed the man who murdered your family . . . the pale one in the cantina."

"Yes, but he was not the man who ordered the raid, the one who planned it and led it. LeCoq did that. His guilt is the greatest of all, and he must pay for what he's done."

"Vengeance is mine, saith the Lord."

"Yes, Father. But as *you* have said, sometimes the Lord uses men as his instruments. Perhaps in this case I can serve as His instrument by ridding the world of these evil men."

"There are too many, and you will be riding right into their camp. You will be killed. "

"It doesn't matter."

"It matters to Señora Beaumont."

"Why do you say that?"

"Several times during the night as she tossed and turned in her sleep she called your name."

"She was delirious."

"She wanted you to be near her, Señor Starbuck."

Starbuck closed his eyes and rubbed his hand over his face. He should not be thinking of Kate Beaumont now. He should be thinking only of the Dark Mountains and of what he must do there. Yet to leave her like this, before she was out of danger. . . .

"I'll stay one more day, Father," he said. "Then I must go."

"If God wills it, my son," said the priest.

When Starbuck returned to Kate Beaumont's room he found that she had awakened from her troubled sleep. As he came through the door she gave him a weak smile and held out her hand to him in welcome. At her insistence he sat beside her and told her of their escape from the plaza, of Diego Fernández' gallant end, and of her own narrow brush with eternity. When she learned of the manner of Fernández' death and that he had died on the doorstep of the very room in which she lay, tears came to her eyes. Still holding tightly to Starbuck's hand she turned her face to the wall and cried quietly for a little while—for Fernández, for her dead husband, for all the things that she had suffered and for all the things that she had lost.

At length she slept again, Starbuck's hand still clutched in hers. When he was certain that she was asleep, he gently disengaged her fingers from his own and slipped from the room. He spent the remainder of the evening prowling wakefully through the mission grounds, rifle in hand, watching and listening.

By the morning of the next day Kate Beaumont was sitting up and taking food. Starbuck had sworn that he would go that morning, yet when he came into her room to take his leave of her he found that he could not bring himself to do it. He told himself that she was still weak, that she still needed him, and that he must stay a little longer for her sake. It did not occur to him that he also needed her, and that his reluctance to go was at least in part a reluctance to say goodbye to her . . . since the goodbye would in all likelihood be forever.

And so he stayed on through another day and another evening, sitting with her, talking with her, sleeping in the chair beside her bed during those portions of the night when he was not pacing silently through the shadowy precincts of the mission.

On the morning of the third day, Starbuck and Father Paul entered the room to find her sitting on the edge of the bed trying painfully to dress herself. Only under protest did she give up the attempt and lie back again upon the pillow. Even then she raised her head up a little and gazed straight at Starbuck, her sunken eyes bright with emotion.

"You're going soon, aren't you?" she said.

"Yes."

"Don't leave without me," she whispered. "Please, Grant—promise me!"

"Just rest, Kate," he said. "Everything will be all right . . . one way or another."

An hour later he found Father Paul praying in the church. The priest raised his head inquiringly.

"I'm sorry to interrupt your prayers, Father," Starbuck said. "Please forgive me."

"It's all right, my son," said the priest. "As it happens, I was praying for you."

He noted the rifle in Starbuck's hand and the saddlebags slung over his shoulder.

"You are going now?" he said.

"Yes, Father. I must. The Señora is better now, and I have an appointment to keep in the Sierra Oscura."

"An appointment with death, I fear."

"Yes."

"Can you not stay another day or two?" said the priest. "Help may be on the way at this very moment. The Mexican officer to whom you wrote the letter. . . ."

"Teniente Guerrero? He has only a few men, Father, and they can't leave the border."

"Your own country's soldiers, then. Perhaps they will come."

"The U.S. Army is forbidden to cross the Rio Bravo. No, Father, there won't be any help. I must go alone."

Starbuck held out a small bag of gold coins.

"Please take this," he said. "It's for the mission. I won't be needing it where I'm going."

The priest shook his head.

"I cannot take your money, my son," he said.

"Please, Father. It's the only way that I can repay you for all that you've done for us."

"I've done nothing for you that I would not have done for anyone in need," the priest said. "Besides, if God has indeed chosen you as His instrument for the punishment of those evil men, then by helping you I have merely been carrying out His wishes. I cannot take money for that."

He raised his hand in benediction.

"Go now, my son, and may God be with you. Return to us if you can."

"Thank you Father," Starbuck said. "I doubt that we'll meet again. Take good care of Mrs. Beaumont, will you?"

"I will, my son. We shall both miss you."

Starbuck saddled his horse and rode south, alone, toward the Dark Mountains.

CHAPTER ELEVEN

Starbuck rode carefully, fully alert to the harsh landscape around him. Twice he left the trail and moved in a wide circle through the broken country, doubling back until he found a hidden spot from which to watch the trail behind him. On each occasion he waited a long time to make certain that he was not being followed before proceeding onward toward the distant foothills.

Sunset found him still far from the mountains, and he camped in the shelter of some boulders well off the trail which he had been following. There was no water and he dared not build a fire, but he was neither cold nor hungry and he had brought water for the horse and for himself. He spent a silent hour cleaning his weapons before rolling himself into his blankets and falling into a restless sleep.

At daybreak he was up again; this time he built a small fire, warmed some coffee, and cooked a little bacon and some beans. He ate the food without relish; his mind was upon what lay ahead of him.

At length he scattered the ashes of the fire and saddled the buckskin. He made another circle to cut his back trail, but there was no sign of pursuit. Whatever he would have to face that day, it was in front of him, not behind him.

The Dark Mountains were well-named. Beyond the smaller foothills the jagged black peaks loomed high above the desert floor, mysterious and forbidding.

As Starbuck entered the first low hills the trail began to climb, gently at first and then more steeply. Soon he was winding upward through a narrow canyon flanked by tall cliffs which towered menacingly over horse and rider, reducing man and beast to insignificance by their massiveness and oppressing the spirit with their brooding presence.

The buckskin picked his way nervously over the loose rocks and shale which littered the trail, at times almost obscuring it. Starbuck let the horse have its head; he was too busy watching the bluffs and the rimrock above to worry about the ground beneath the stallion's feet. The trail became steeper and narrower, and the vaulting cliffs shut off more and more of the light.

The somber mood of the place might have touched another man, casting a chill upon even the stoutest heart. But Starbuck's heart was too full of hatred to be much affected by the melancholy atmosphere; he rode doggedly on, alert for danger but single-mindedly intent upon his purpose. Ahead—close ahead— lay the hiding-place of those who had destroyed everything that he loved, and there was no longer room in his soul for anything except his consuming desire for retribution. He longed savagely for the joy of reprisal, the fulfillment of vengeance. Now and then he urged the buckskin forward at a faster pace, fearful that death might overtake him before he reached his goal.

Gradually Starbuck became aware that he was being watched. No sight, no sound came to him at first, yet he could feel the unfriendly eyes fixed upon him, the hostile presence in the rocks. Involuntarily he tensed his muscles, bracing himself for the bullet which would fling him dying into the dust of the trail, but it did not come. He rode on, waiting.

Suddenly he became aware of a shadow on the skyline above him. A man was standing on the rimrock, sombrero in one hand, rifle in the other, observing his approach. Starbuck started to draw his Winchester from its scabbard, then hesitated. The man on the rim was making no attempt to hide himself, nor was he making any move to raise his own rifle to a firing position. He just stood there as if carved in stone. Starbuck glanced quickly at the other side of the canyon and saw another rifleman leaning easily against a boulder at the top of the cliff, gazing motionless in Starbuck's direction. Starbuck kept the buckskin moving, expecting the men to kill him, but they remained still, letting him pass by.

Thereafter, each twist of the canyon revealed another sentinel in the rocks, each of them motionless, alert, watching. As he rounded still another bend he found one such sentry, a Mexican, standing atop a large boulder just a few feet from the trail, his rifle resting carelessly across his shoulder. Starbuck instinctively reined up, bracing himself for combat, but the man merely smiled and gave an exaggerated bow, sweeping his sombrero before him in a sarcastic invitation to Starbuck to proceed past him up the trail.

Now a chill began to settle upon Starbuck's heart, for he knew that all of his options were gone; there was nothing left for him to do but to ride on into the mountains under the eyes of these silent sentries. His presence was known, his coming was expected. At the head of the trail he would find what he had come for . . . and what he had come for would find him.

Ahead, two sharp stones rose like fangs beside the trail, one on each side, forming a gate in the rocks. On each side of the gate was a mounted rifleman, guarding the entrance. Starbuck thought again of the name given by the Indians to this place— Guarida Diablo. He passed the horsemen and the rocks, riding alone into the Devil's Lair.

Beyond the gateway the trail crested and started down, widening out into a small valley hemmed in on all sides by what appeared to be impenetrable cliffs. Rude buildings of gray-black stone filled the valley, some of them quite large. Starbuck realized that he was entering a primitive village, its homes, stables, and storehouses all made from the rock of the surrounding hills. Smoke rose from crude stone fireplaces dotted here and there among the buildings, and he saw groups of dirty women gathered near the fireplaces, staring at him with wide, dark eyes. Naked children, dirtier still, peered fearfully from behind the women's skirts.

The encampment was as filthy as the people in it; garbage of all sorts was strewn about the open areas and piled in stinking heaps against the walls of the buildings. A pack of huge, half-starved dogs was foraging among the offal; two of them ran past Starbuck, snarling and snapping as they fought for possession of a shriveled, leathery object which they had found. Starbuck's stomach turned over as he saw that it was a severed human hand.

But he had little time to spare for such minor matters. Something far more ominous than women, dirt, and dogs lay ahead. As he came through the encampment he found himself confronted by a body of horsemen, perhaps fifteen or twenty of them, drawn up into two lines which stretched out on either side of the trail in front of him for a hundred yards or more. His arrival had been foreseen; the riders had formed a gauntlet, and they were waiting for him to pass along it. Most of them were holding rifles at the ready, while a few lounged forward in their saddles, pistols held carelessly in their hands. Would they kill him as he rode between them, or did they have something more exotic in mind? He glanced back briefly, but there was to be no retreat; other horsemen had closed in behind him.

Oddly, he felt no fear; instead, a strange elation gripped him, as he realized that all that he had come for was now within his grasp. This was what he had ridden so far to attain. He had kept his appointment with death.

He reined in the buckskin, reached into his shirt pocket, and took out the marshal's star. Carefully he pinned the badge above his left shirt pocket. Then he nudged the buckskin forward again toward the waiting riders.

Unhurriedly he guided his mount up through the double line of horsemen. As he rode he examined them dispassionately. There were men of all descriptions there, whites and Indians, Americans and Mexicans, the sort of mixture that one would expect in such a place. Yet Starbuck knew that there was one thing that they would have in common. They would all be outcasts, outlaws, killers . . . granite-hard men, without morals, hope, or pity, the kind of men who would destroy anything—an animal, a human being, or an entire town—without the slightest compunction. And all of them were watching him with malevolent anticipation.

He ignored them, for he saw immediately the purpose of the gauntlet and understood what he was expected to do. At the head of the double line of horsemen a solitary figure stood alone, hands on hips, eyes gleaming expectantly out of the shadow cast by his ornate sombrero.

Starbuck walked the buckskin up to the man and reined in, looking down at him.

"Welcome, Señor Marshal," said the man, grinning broadly. "We have been expecting you, as you can see." He was a large man, fat, with little pig-like eyes and a drooping, food-stained mustache.

"Are you LeCoq?" Starbuck said.

The fat man put back his head and laughed.

"Ah, no, Señor," he said. "I am Escobar. I am Comandante LeCoq's . . . how do you gringos say it . . . 'right-hand man.'"

"Then take me to him," Starbuck said.

"But of course, Señor," said Escobar with elaborate irony. "The Comandante has been anxiously awaiting your arrival. Perhaps you will be kind enough to dismount and follow me?"

He laughed again, then started up a rocky path toward a large stone house set into the side of the hill above them. Starbuck got down off the buckskin; a man whose appearance was as repulsive as his odor stepped forward and took the reins from his hand, leering at him. Starbuck started to reach across the saddle for his Winchester, but the man shook his hand meaningfully, raising his pistol. Starbuck smiled bleakly and followed Escobar up the hill. Four of the horsemen dismounted and fell in behind him, their pistols swinging loosely in their hands.

"Here is something that may interest you, Señor Marshal," Escobar said, pausing in his stride.

A pair of posts had been planted close beside the path; each timber was set deep into the ground and slanted so that the two posts formed an upright "X." Upon this structure a man was spreadeagled, his wrists and ankles bound to the posts by rawhide thongs; his eyes were glazed and he was only semi-conscious. He had been stripped naked to the waist, and the sun had burned deeply into his unprotected skin. His face, shoulders, and chest were a mass of blisters, and the skin had peeled away in places revealing the bloody flesh beneath.

"Water," he croaked. "For the love of God, give me water."

"What's this?" Starbuck said to Escobar. The Mexican shrugged.

"Just a man," he said. "At least he used to be a man."

"Where did you capture him?"

"Capture him?" Escobar seemed puzzled by the question at first, then smiled as understanding dawned.

"We did not capture him," he said, grinning. "That is Murphy. He is one of our own men."

"But why. . . . ?"

"He broke the law. Our law. He stole something that belonged to one of his comrades. That is not permitted here. Comandante LeCoq is very strict about such matters . . . as you see."

"How long have you had him tied up there like that?"

"Three days. They usually die within a day or two. The sun and the lack of water, you understand. But Murphy is a strong man, stronger than most. Still, he will be dead by tomorrow morning, I think."

He beamed at Starbuck.

"Do you use such methods to enforce the law in your town of Comanche Wells, Señor Marshal?"

"Hardly," said Starbuck, fighting back the revulsion which rose up in him as he regarded the suffering man. Even an outlaw did not deserve to die like that.

Escobar saw the expression on Starbuck's face and gave him another bright smile.

"Do not feel too sorry for him, my friend," he said. "Who knows . . . perhaps by this evening you will have joined him, eh?"

Starbuck saw that there were other sets of posts scattered around the area, but these were empty. Dried blood streaked the wood, and rawhide thongs hung loosely from the timbers, waiting.

"Were you there . . . at Comanche Wells?" he said.

"But of course," said Escobar. "It was a most pleasant morning."

He slapped Starbuck on the shoulder.

"I hear that the Señora Beaumont is now your traveling companion," he said. "You should thank me for making her a widow for you, no?"

"You were at the Beaumont ranch too?"

"Indeed, yes. I killed Señor Beaumont myself. But it was very careless of me to overlook the Señora's presence. I hear that she is a very handsome woman, and I would have enjoyed entertaining her."

Starbuck struggled to conceal his anger.

"What have you done with the women that you took from Comanche Wells?" he said.

"Those silly cows?" said Escobar making a wry face. "They were weak and of little use to us. Only four of them lived to see our little community here."

"Where are the four now?"

"Oh, they are all dead," Escobar said offhandedly. "We used them until they were no longer enjoyable, and then we fed them to the dogs."

Starbuck remembered the two hungry mongrels fighting over the severed hand. The bile rose in his throat, but he kept his expression blank. Escobar was watching him with amusement, and Starbuck would not give him the satisfaction of seeing the disgust which filled him.

Disappointed at Starbuck's lack of reaction, Escobar turned and proceeded up the path. Looking at the man's fat back moving ahead of him, Starbuck resolved that before he died he would make certain that, like his chief, Escobar would pay in blood for the agony of Comanche Wells.

They climbed a series of steps carved out of the living rock of the hillside and emerged upon a broad patio in front of the house. Escobar removed his sombrero and knocked loudly on the heavy wooden door of the house, then swung it open and gestured for Starbuck to enter.

The interior of the house was cool and well lit by the sun streaming in through the open windows. The room was furnished with pieces crafted in the Spanish style. A rug covered the flagstone floor; paintings hung upon the wall, and there were several sculptures in evidence.

"So," said a silky voice, "this is the famous Marshal Starbuck."

The speaker was standing in a doorway at one end of the room. He was tall, thin, dressed entirely in black. In one hand he was holding a half-filled brandy glass, while with the other he was alternately caressing the two young women who were leaning against him, giggling and running their hands over his body. The blouse of one of the women was pulled far down, revealing her right breast. She made no attempt to cover herself as she gazed lewdly at Starbuck.

But Starbuck paid no attention to the women; he was studying the black-clad man intently, noting the hawk-like face, the cruel eyes, and the livid scar which ran across the man's left cheek. It was the description which the survivors of Comanche Wells had given of the leader of the massacre.

Starbuck felt the wrath rising within him.

"Is your name Pierre LeCoq?" he rasped.

The man bowed mockingly.

"*Comandante* Pierre LeCoq," he said, "at your service."

He pushed the women away from him, propelling them back through the doorway.

"Wait for me in the bedroom, my pets," he murmured, handing one of them the brandy snifter. "I will not be detained for very long."

"Now, Monsieur," he said, facing Starbuck again, "To what do I owe the honor of this visit?"

"You led the raid on Comanche Wells?"

"But of course. The town burned most satisfactorily, don't you think?"

"And the attack on the Beaumont ranch?"

"I ordered it—that and others. Many others. Why?"

"You're under arrest," Starbuck said.

Escobar and the four gunmen guffawed loudly. LeCoq merely smiled.

"Monsieur," he said coldly, "you are either a very brave man or a complete fool. In either case you have come a long way just to die. You will never leave this place alive."

"Perhaps," said Starbuck. "But you're still under arrest."

LeCoq's smile faded.

"After my men told me about the incident in the cantina, I was curious about you, Monsieur Starbuck," he said. "So when I heard that you were on your way here I decided to let you live long enough that I might have the pleasure of meeting you. I must say that I am not disappointed. You are unique."

"You talk too much," Starbuck said. "I can shoot you now or hang you later. Take your choice."

He moved his hand down to his side, near the ivory handle of the Colt.

"Surely you do not intend to try to draw on me, Marshal," said LeCoq. "Escobar and four of my soldiers are standing right behind you with their pistols pointed at your back. If you were to so much as touch that weapon at your side you would be dead within the instant." He snickered.

"Such bravado. I would admire it if it were not so stupid."

Carefully, using his left hand, Starbuck slid a pair of handcuffs out of his belt and tossed them on the floor in front of LeCoq.

"Put them on, LeCoq. Or go for your gun."

An expression of amused contempt crossed LeCoq's face.

"But I am unarmed, my dear Marshal. Would you shoot down a defenseless man?"

"You've got a derringer in your right boot," Starbuck said. "I can see it from here. Use it . . . or put on the handcuffs."

"You are very observant," said LeCoq with an approving nod. "But I would have little chance with a mere derringer against you and your Colt Peacemaker."

"Then get your six-gun," said Starbuck. "Get a shotgun. Get a Gatling gun if you like. But get it *now*, you sadistic bastard. You're running out of time."

Anger darkened LeCoq's features.

"*I* am running out of time?" he sneered. "How droll. I tell you again that you are a dead man, Monsieur. You have been dead since you first dared to ride into these mountains."

"What's the matter?" Starbuck said. "Afraid you're too slow on the draw? Or is it just that you don't want these scum you call your 'soldiers' to find out that you're yellow?"

LeCoq shook his head in wonder.

"Astonishing, is it not, Escobar?" he said. "The man is deliberately taunting me. He is trying to goad me into fighting a duel with him, as if we were two rowdies facing each other in the streets of some dirty little Texas cowtown."

"Let me kill him, Comandante!" said Escobar with a grin.

"No," said LeCoq. "No, I don't think so. . . ."

He regarded Starbuck speculatively.

"I ought to have you tied to the stakes outside and let you rot in the sun," he mused, "but . . . I think that I see an opportunity here for a bit of entertainment. Something a little out of the ordinary. Escobar, how many of the men who raided Comanche Wells are still with us?"

"Very few, Comandante. We have lost so many in the past few days. Some in Texas, more at the Rio Bravo, many more in the cantina." He did a quick count on his fingers.

"Dios mio," he mumbled. "There are only three left, Comandante. Besides ourselves, of course."

"Only three?" said LeCoq. "From among so many? Mon Dieu! All right, who are they?"

"Ramirez, Williamson, and Danziger."

"Ah, yes. Well, they will have to do. Have them come up to the patio."

He walked over to a rack on the wall, took down a gunbelt from a peg, and strapped it on. The black holster sheathed an ornately engraved nickel-plated revolver with mother-of-pearl handles. LeCoq drew the six-gun and leveled it at Starbuck's chest.

Starbuck's muscles tensed involuntarily. LeCoq saw the movement.

"Do not worry," he sniggered. "I am not going to kill you. Not just yet."

He motioned toward the door.

"Outside, Monsieur Marshal," he said. "We are going to find out just how brave you really are."

CHAPTER TWELVE

They herded him out of the door at gunpoint and stood him at one end of the flagstoned terrace in front of the house. Three men came climbing sullenly up the steps, their eyes shifting from Starbuck to LeCoq and back again. When they had reached the top of the stairs, LeCoq ordered them to stand at the opposite end of the terrace. LeCoq, Escobar, and the four "soldiers" stood against the wall of the house well clear of Starbuck and the three newcomers. Below, at the foot of the steps, the rest of LeCoq's men had gathered—perhaps thirty of them altogether. They had dismounted from their horses and were staring expectantly up at the scene on the terrace, elbowing each other knowingly and exchanging jovial comments.

"Now, my vengeful friend," LeCoq said, "you have ridden far to find the men who set fire to your silly little town. Very well, you have found us. So now I am going to give you your chance."

He smirked at Starbuck, then gestured at the three gunmen at the other end of the terrace.

"You wish to arrest someone, my dear Marshal?" he said. "Very well, let us see if you can arrest *them!*"

Starbuck inspected the three men carefully. They were as rough-looking as any of the rest of LeCoq's cutthroats, and they were each carrying a revolver; one of them, the man called Danziger, was wearing two. Three men to one, four guns to one. And the range was short—not more than twenty feet. With three experienced gunmen firing at him at that distance, it was unlikely that Starbuck would survive long enough to kill all of them, much less have a chance to get LeCoq afterwards.

Starbuck decided that there was only one thing for him to do. He would have to kill LeCoq first, then get as many of the others as he could before he went down. He told himself that if he could just kill LeCoq before Escobar and the rest cut him down, he would die content.

But LeCoq had anticipated him.

"Escobar," he said, "listen to me very carefully. You and your men are to keep your weapons aimed at Marshal Starbuck. If he fires at anyone besides our three friends over there—for example, if he allows the muzzle of his revolver to stray in my direction— you will kill him instantly."

He stared malevolently at Starbuck.

"Furthermore, Escobar," he said, "if despite your precautions the Marshal should somehow manage to injure or kill me, these are my orders: You will immediately take the men and ride into Pueblo Rojo. There you will destroy the mission and crucify the priests on their own altar, after which you will bring the Beaumont woman back here."

"And then, Comandante?" said Escobar eagerly.

"You and the men may use her however you like for as long as you like."

"Ah," said Escobar. "And when we are through with her we will give her to the dogs, yes?"

"No," said LeCoq. "You will not give her to the dogs."

Escobar looked crestfallen.

"But, Comandante, what are we to do with her when we get tired of her?"

"You will burn her," LeCoq replied. "Do you hear me, Escobar? If Starbuck harms me in any way, the woman is to be burned alive."

CHARLES E. FRIEND

"Yes, Comandante," Escobar said, beaming with pleasure. "I will attend to it personally."

"See that you do," said LeCoq.

He gave Starbuck a wicked smile.

"Do you understand the rules of our little game, Marshal?" he said.

"I understand, all right," Starbuck growled. The mere thought of what LeCoq had threatened nauseated him. Whatever the cost, he could not let it happen. He must fight the three gunmen, and be content with that. He could not kill LeCoq after all.

It's true, he thought. I've come a long way just to die.

"Are you ready, Marshal?" said LeCoq cheerfully.

Starbuck shrugged.

"Good," said LeCoq. He looked at the three gunmen at the end of the terrace. "You three," he said, "listen to me. This arrogant American lawman has come to arrest you—if he can. Now, I am going to count to three. After that, those of you who prefer not to be arrested may kill him by whatever means pleases you."

He held up a shining coin.

"And, to make it more interesting," he said, "I am offering this hundred-dollar gold piece to the first man who puts a bullet through that ridiculous metal star that the Marshal is wearing on his shirt. Is all of this clear to you? Splendid. Now, if you are ready, we will begin. One . . . two. . . ."

On the count of two, Danziger went for his guns. Starbuck was ready; he had not expected these men to fight according to any set of rules. Nevertheless, Danziger had gained a momentary advantage by his treachery. His hands were already on the handles of his weapons by the time that Starbuck could react.

But Danziger's choice of a simultaneous two-gun draw was a poor one; no such action could be as fast as that of an experienced man drawing one weapon at a time. The barrels of the outlaw's six-guns were just clearing the tops of their twin holsters when Starbuck's Colt bucked in his hand, sending a .45 slug slamming into Danziger's chest. The gunman's two weapons clattered to the stones unfired as he went down.

119

The second man, Ramirez, had waited longer to begin his draw but he was faster than Danziger. As Starbuck swung the muzzle of the Colt toward him, Ramirez' Remington .44 barked once. Starbuck, knowing the outlaw was going to get off a shot, twisted his body to the left; the bullet sliced across the front of his stomach, tearing the flesh but not penetrating the abdomen. Ignoring the searing pain, Starbuck shot Ramirez through the lungs and kept the Colt's muzzle swinging toward the last man, Williamson, whose pistol was just coming up.

Their guns roared simultaneously, and Williamson's bullet slammed into Starbuck's thigh, knocking his leg from under him and dropping him to his knees on the stones of the terrace. It was Williamson's last earthly act, however, for Starbuck's first bullet broke his pelvis and the second hit him squarely between the eyes. He fell disjointedly, dead before his body touched the blood-spattered stones of the terrace.

Starbuck knelt on the flagstones holding his smoking Colt in one hand while he pressed his left arm against his injured stomach. He waited for the impact of the bullets which must surely come now from LeCoq, Escobar, and the others.

"Mother of God!" exclaimed Escobar, staring at the three dead men. "He got all of them."

"Amazing," said LeCoq. "I would not have thought it possible."

He walked over to where Starbuck was kneeling on the stones and bent down, lowering his voice so that the men standing at the foot of the terrace could not hear him. There was a crooked smile on his lips. "I fear that you have put me in a very awkward position," Monsieur," he murmured. "I did not expect you to kill all three of them. You have embarrassed me in front of my men, and I cannot afford that. Now it appears that I shall have to dispose of you myself."

Something in his voice made Starbuck look sharply up at him. LeCoq's breathing was becoming more rapid, and there was a strange glitter in his eyes. It was obvious that he was excited by the idea of dispatching Starbuck personally.

"Can you stand?" LeCoq asked solicitously.

"For the chance to kill you, I'd fly," Starbuck gasped, struggling to his feet. His stomach burned like fire, and his left leg almost buckled when he put his weight on it. Blood was coursing down his leg, but at least the bone was not broken. Ignoring the pain, he started to shove new cartridges into the Colt's cylinder. Escobar reached over and gripped his wrist tightly.

"That will not be necessary, Señor," he said. "You still have two bullets left in the pistola. That is enough." He guided the Colt back into Starbuck's holster.

"Yes," said LeCoq. "In fact, that may be too many. I am reasonably proficient with firearms, Marshal, but you are just a little too fast with that Colt for my liking. I think that we had better even up the odds a bit more. Escobar!"

Escobar stepped up behind Starbuck, holding a rifle by the barrel. Before Starbuck could move, Escobar swung the rifle with all of his strength in a sweeping, vicious arc; the butt of the rifle slammed into Starbuck's right arm above the elbow, breaking the bone. Agony knifed through him, and he fell heavily, trying not to cry out as he clutched at the broken arm with his left hand.

"Get him up," said LeCoq. His eyes were shining now, and his breathing was very heavy. Starbuck saw with disgust that the man was actually physically aroused by what he had just witnessed.

Escobar and one of the others pulled Starbuck to his feet. He nearly fainted with the pain as they hauled him up, but he managed to stay conscious and to remain standing when Escobar and the other man released him and stepped aside.

"Excellent," said LeCoq.

"But Comandante," said Escobar, "how will he draw the pistola now? The men will be so disappointed. . . ."

"That is easily arranged," said LeCoq smugly. "Pull his gunbelt around so that the holster is on the left side. Then if he likes he can draw left-handed. You still have a perfectly good left arm, haven't you Marshal?"

They tugged the belt around Starbuck's body so that the holster was against his left thigh. Escobar reached down and reversed the Colt so that it sat awkwardly in the holster with its butt now to the left rear. The Mexican chuckled at its comical appearance.

"You expect me to draw on you?" said Starbuck to LeCoq. He was swaying on his feet.

"You may do so if you wish," LeCoq said, "but it doesn't matter. I will kill you whether you draw or not."

"But if I do . . . what about the priests and the woman? You said that if I injured you, you'd have them killed."

"Oh, that," said LeCoq indifferently. "I am going to have them killed anyway, regardless of what you do. Did you really think I would let them go after all their meddling?" He shook his head. "You really *are* a fool."

Rage welled up in Starbuck. He should have killed LeCoq when he had the chance. Now. . . .

He looked down at the Colt jammed awkwardly into the holster on his left side.

"And this is your idea of a fair fight?" he said.

"I am not interested in being fair," LeCoq replied. "I am only interested in killing you. But we will make a little show of this, you and I. We will *pretend* that it is a fair fight. It will entertain my men, and I will enjoy it. Yes, I think that I will enjoy it very much." He licked his lips in anticipation. "You may draw whenever you please, Marshal," he said.

With an immense effort of the will, Starbuck fought off the pain and the swirling darkness which had been about to swallow him up. Perhaps it was just the imminence of death, or perhaps it was the bitter hatred rising within him once more which gave him the strength to face this final ordeal. Or perhaps the surge of power derived from another, higher source. Whatever the reason, suddenly his mind was clear again, the pain forgotten as he confronted LeCoq—the murderer who had destroyed his home and family, the sadistic monster who derived sexual pleasure from the suffering of others.

Slowly Starbuck pulled himself erect, gathering himself for this one last effort.

LeCoq mistook the delay for fear.

"You will not fight?" he sneered. "A pity. It would have been so much more amusing that way. But the result will be the same."

LeCoq's breath was coming in quick gasps now, and his eyes were glazed.

"Good-bye, Monsieur Starbuck," he said.

As he reached for his nickel-plated six-gun, a little moan of pleasure escaped his lips.

Starbuck's left hand flashed up past his twisted holster, bringing the Colt with it. The movement was swift and precise—the hammer of the Colt was already in the cocked position as the six-gun cleared the holster, the muzzle aimed instantly and unwaveringly at LeCoq's midsection.

LeCoq froze, gaping at Starbuck in horrified disbelief. Starbuck's draw had been so fast that the Frenchman had not even had time to touch the handle of his own weapon.

"But . . . but you are right-handed!" he stammered. "Your gun-arm is broken!"

Starbuck's soul filled with a savage elation as he saw the fear spring up in LeCoq's eyes. He bared his teeth in a mirthless smile.

"You made a mistake, LeCoq," he said. "A fatal one. Firearms are the tools of my trade. Surely you didn't think that I could only use a gun with one hand?"

He laughed. "You should have broken both of my arms, you murdering bastard."

He shoved the muzzle of the Colt hard into the flesh of LeCoq's abdomen, just below the belt buckle.

"Wait!" cried LeCoq. "Do not shoot! We can come to terms! I am a rich man, a very rich man. . . ."

"Not rich enough, my friend," Starbuck said. "Not nearly rich enough."

He leaned forward, pressing the barrel of the gun still deeper into LeCoq's belly.

"This is for my family," he whispered.

LeCoq screamed in terror and clawed desperately for his own weapon, but it was far too late.

Starbuck shot him twice through the body. The first explosion tore open LeCoq's abdomen and ripped into his entrails; the muzzle flash set his shirt afire. The second bullet slammed through his remaining organs and shattered his spine.

Instantly the Frenchman's paralyzed legs collapsed beneath him and he crashed helplessly to the terrace. He lay there, writhing grotesquely and squealing like a pig, as his intestines poured out of his ruptured belly onto the flagstones. Blood and viscera quickly quenched the burning shirt.

Starbuck watched LeCoq's death agonies dispassionately, knowing that the moment of victory would be brief. His six-gun was empty—he had fired both of the last two rounds into LeCoq, leaving himself defenseless. Now the other outlaws would surely kill him. Slowly he turned to face Escobar, the useless Colt dangling at his side.

Fortunately for Starbuck, Escobar had momentarily forgotten him. The Mexican was standing as if stupefied, gawking down at LeCoq in open-mouthed incomprehension as the dying outlaw chieftain lay screaming at his feet.

Then, as the reality of what had happened dawned upon Escobar, he whirled toward Starbuck, his eyes blazing with fury. His features contorted wildly, and spittle flew from his lips.

"You gringo scum!" he howled. "You filthy son of a whore! You'll pay for this, you. . . ."

Bellowing obscenities, the Mexican lunged forward and raised his revolver until its muzzle was a scant six inches from Starbuck's face. Starbuck could clearly see the rifling in the barrel of the weapon, and the dull gleam of the heavy soft-nosed bullets waiting in their chambers.

The pain of his injuries had now become so intense that he was close to fainting again. He struggled to remain conscious, but there was a roaring in his ears and everything seemed to be growing dark. He swayed, trying not to fall; he was determined that if he must die he would die on his feet, defiant and unflinching. The last thing that he saw as he prepared himself for the end was Escobar's twisted face leering at him over the barrel of the six-gun.

Escobar cocked the revolver.

The boom of the Sharps rifle filled the valley, echoing violently back and forth among the rocks. The heavy .52-caliber bullet whipped past Starbuck's ear and struck Escobar squarely in the throat, tearing away his larynx and ripping open the trachea. The fat outlaw staggered backwards, blood spurting from the ruptured arteries. He dropped his pistol and sank to his knees, clawing frantically at the remains of his throat. As Starbuck watched, Escobar's eyes bulged slowly out of his head, and he began to make strange gargling sounds. Then he fell squirming onto the flagstones, strangling in his own blood.

Starbuck looked around, stunned. Every man, woman, and child in the valley was gaping in astonishment at the rocky entrance to the encampment, for it was from there that the unexpected gunshot had come. Starbuck's heart leaped as he grasped what was happening.

The camp was under attack. Dozens of mounted men were charging through the gateway in the rocks, yelling like madmen and firing their rifles indiscriminately at anything which moved in front of them.

Yet it was not the oncoming horsemen that captured Starbuck's attention. Instead, he found himself staring at a little mule-drawn cart that had suddenly appeared near the entrance to the camp. On the back of the cart a tall woman with copper-colored hair was standing calmly upright, ignoring the battle exploding around her. An elderly man in a flowing robe stood beside her, supporting her with his arm. There was a halo of gunsmoke around the woman's head, and she was already slamming another cartridge into the breech of the Sharps cavalry carbine which she was holding before her, its muzzle still pointed at the terrace.

Despite his pain, despite the swirling dust and drifting powder smoke which half-obscured his view, Starbuck recognized the woman instantly. It was Kate Beaumont.

And around her, around the wagon upon which she stood, around the rocks and the stone houses and over anything else that got in their way, the attackers came storming—fifty of them or more, spurring their excited horses headlong into the encampment, shouting like madmen as they thundered down upon the startled bandits gathered at the foot of the terrace.

For a fleeting instant LeCoq's men remained motionless, immobilized by shock; then they reacted, scattering in all directions and firing back at the attackers as they ran. Dazed and sick, Starbuck could only stand there, clinging to his empty Colt and watching helplessly as attackers and defenders collided, exchanged fire, cursed, screamed, and died.

But the outcome of the assault was never in doubt. The outlaws had been bunched on foot below the terrace, distracted by the encounter between Starbuck and LeCoq and totally unprepared for a sudden assault upon their stronghold. They fought back desperately, but they were disorganized and heavily outnumbered. Within moments half of them lay on the ground dead or dying, while the rest were being cut down by flying lead as they ran for cover. A few made it to the walls of nearby buildings, but the galloping horsemen swept around the corners in a body, tearing the last of the bandits apart with a withering fire.

The attackers were all in civilian clothes, but to Starbuck's fevered imagination there was something familiar about the way that they rode and fought, the shouted commands, the heavy Sharps carbines. . . .

Gunfire erupted behind Starbuck. The four outlaws who had been on the terrace when the attack began had recovered from their amazement and joined the fight. One was already hit, down on his knees and out of action, but the other three were shooting at the attackers. One of them saw Starbuck and swung his pistol toward the crouching lawman. Starbuck dropped his empty Colt and seized the nickel-plated revolver which had fallen from LeCoq's dying hand to the flagstones in front of him. The bandit fired at Starbuck, but his aim was faulty and he was given no second chance. Starbuck killed him with one shot. He fired at the next outlaw, missed, and shot again; this time the bullet carried away part of the man's skull.

Starbuck shifted his aim to deal with the remaining bandit, but it proved to be unnecessary. One of the attacking horsemen had charged his mount up the hill and onto the terrace; he dispatched the last gunman with a sweeping cut of his saber. With a sickening thud the blade drove deep into the doomed man's neck and shoulder, nearly splitting him in half. The man shrieked and died.

The saber-wielding horseman wheeled his mount and brought it clattering across the stones, reining up alongside Starbuck. Starbuck stared up at the rider as he towered there on the prancing horse, silhouetted against the blazing sun. The horseman was wearing a buckskin shirt and dark blue trousers . . . trousers from which something, some sort of stripe, had recently been torn.

"Hello, Grant," said the silhouette. "Didn't really expect to see you again. Can't be too many of your nine lives left."

It was Sam Lattimer.

Starbuck sank slowly to his knees, the strength draining out of him.

"Hello, Sam," he said weakly. "Out of uniform, aren't you?"

The firing in the encampment below them had stopped. Looking out across the valley as he knelt there on the terrace, Starbuck could see that all resistance had ceased. The attackers were still milling around searching for targets, but there were none to be found. All of the bandits lay sprawled upon the hard and bloodied ground, dead or dying.

Lattimer swung down from his horse and put his arm around Starbuck's shoulders. Starbuck winced; with the fighting madness now fading, the pain was coming back.

"Good heavens, man," said Lattimer, "you're a mess. What did you do? Try to take them all on at once?"

"Just one at a time, Sam" said Starbuck. "Just one at a time."

Another horseman spurred his horse up the slope onto the terrace and dismounted to kneel beside him.

"Señor Starbuck! Gracias a Dios that you are alive," cried Teniente Roberto Guerrero. "Are you badly hurt?"

"He's busted up some," Lattimer said, "but he'll make it. This hombre's too ornery to let a mere couple of dozen bandidos kill him. He'll probably die in bed of boredom when he's a hundred and five."

Starbuck's head was spinning; the faintness was overwhelming him again.

"Kate," he murmured. "Where's Kate?"

"She's back there in the wagon," said Lattimer. "Father Paul and about six troopers are holding her down so she won't come running up here to see if you're still in one piece."

"I'll send one of my men to tell her that you are all right," said Guerrero.

"But how did she get here?" said Starbuck. "How did all of you get here?"

"Well," said Lattimer, "a funny thing happened when D Troop got back to Fort Scott after the fight at the river. The whole damned troop resigned from the Army. Just up and resigned. Would you believe it?"

"No," said Starbuck. "I wouldn't."

Lattimer grinned.

"As a matter of fact," he said, "the resignations were sort of temporary. The Colonel's got the papers in his bottom desk drawer and they'll all mysteriously get 'lost' when we get back to the Fort. But officially and for the record, when we crossed the Rio Grande again yesterday we were just a bunch of no-account, out-of-work civilians coming south for a little Mexican vacation."

He surveyed Starbuck's wounds and shook his head.

"Lie back now," he said, "and let us do a little repair work on you. You look awful."

They eased him back onto the flagstones. Lattimer removed his own neckerchief and tied it tightly around the wound in Starbuck's thigh.

"We decided that the best way to start our vacation was to drop by the garrison at Rio del Norte and say hello to Lieutenant Guerrero here," Lattimer continued. "He'd just gotten your letter. We talked about it over a couple of bottles of tequila, and the next thing you know a bunch of the Lieutenant's men decided they had a bit of leave coming to them. So they shucked their uniforms and all of us ex-army types did a little hard riding toward Pueblo Rojo."

Lieutenant Guerrero had unwound a long sash from his waist and was binding up Starbuck's bleeding stomach.

"We found Señora Beaumont at the mission," he said. "She was very upset that you had left without her. When she found out what we were going to do, she refused to stay behind."

He shook his head in awe.

"She is a very determined woman, that one."

"But she's hurt," said Starbuck. "How could she travel?"

"She made us put her on a mattress in the good Father's little cart," replied Guerrero. "Father Paul said he couldn't let her go alone, so he came along also. It must have been a very rough ride for her, but all the while she kept shouting to us to hurry."

"But the sentries along the trail," said Starbuck. "How did you get past them?"

Lattimer was fashioning a crude splint for Starbuck's broken arm.

"John Two Trees and his scouts got them," he said. "Not a single one of 'em lived long enough to raise the alarm. When we came through that little pass back there a minute ago and cut loose, those bandidos thought they were seeing ghosts, they were so surprised. You should have seen their faces."

"I did," said Starbuck. "I was a damn sight closer to them than you were."

Lattimer finished tying the splint.

"There," he grunted, "that'll hold that arm until we can get it properly attended to. Seems like a clean break. You'll play the violin again."

"Help me up," said Starbuck. He held onto his injured arm with his good hand, gritting his teeth as he struggled to his feet. The two officers started to assist him toward the steps leading down from the terrace, but he stopped them.

"Wait," he said. "There's something else I have to do."

"What is it?" asked Lattimer.

"Can somebody find me some coal oil?"

"Coal oil?"

"Yes."

Guerrero sent one of his men into the house. A few moments later the soldier came back out again with an armful of oil lamps.

Starbuck took the lamps one by one and poured their contents over the bodies of LeCoq and Escobar.

"Now wait a minute, Grant. . . ." Lattimer began.

"Got a match, Sam?" Starbuck said. His eyes were like flint.

Lattimer silently handed him the match.

Starbuck lit it and dropped it into the pool of kerosene between the two corpses. Fire leaped up, the flames rapidly engulfing the bodies. Smoke curled upward as the two men's clothing caught fire, and presently the smell of burning flesh began to drift across the terrace.

Starbuck stood silently watching LeCoq and Escobar burn, his face expressionless. It occurred to him that he should be feeling something at this moment—triumph, perhaps, or at least some sort of satisfaction—but he found to his surprise that instead there was only a great emptiness within him.

At last, when the two bodies were scorched and shriveled beyond recognition, he lowered his head and turned away.

"All right," he said. "We can go now."

With Guerrero and Lattimer helping him he made his way slowly down the hill, then limped through the litter of dead and dying outlaws toward the spot where the little cart was standing.

Kate Beaumont was there, kneeling in the bed of the cart with Father Paul beside her. There was blood seeping through her shirt from her wound, but it was only a small stain, and she was in the process of pushing away Father Paul's supporting arm and climbing out of the cart even as Starbuck approached.

When she saw him coming her eyes lit up, and she hurriedly

slid down out of the cart and stumbled forward, reaching out for him.

"Thank God," she said, throwing her arms around him and resting her head against his chest. "Thank God."

Starbuck encircled her shoulders with his good arm. Her hair was soft against his cheek.

"You shouldn't have come, Kate," he said. "Are you all right?"

"Yes, I'm all right . . . now," she murmured. "I said I'd be in at the finish, Grant. I said I'd see them die. And I did. I'm so glad I did. The one I shot—was he. . . . ?"

"You got the right man, Kate. He was at Comanche Wells and he led the attack on your ranch. He would have killed me if you hadn't nailed him."

"Damn good shot, too," said Lattimer, admiringly. "By God, Grant, that's some woman you've got there. If I were twenty years younger. . . ."

"She's not my woman," Starbuck said, a note of sadness in his voice.

Kate Beaumont tightened her arms around his body and looked up at him, her green eyes flashing.

"The hell I'm not," she said.

THE END